POWER PLAY

Jessica was stunned. "Robin Wilson in Pi Beta Alpha? With *us*? With Lila Fowler? One look at that shape and they'll be calling us the Pi *Butterball* Alphas! Oh, really, Liz, are you completely absent from this universe?"

Elizabeth sighed. "Jessica, for heaven's sake, don't come unglued. I've promised, and that's that. Robin Wilson's going to be in the sorority."

"Oh, is she?"

"Look," Elizabeth said, "if I sponsor Robin, and you're the president of Pi Beta Alpha—*and* her best friend—she's in."

Jessica's only response was to toss her head and stomp out of the room. It wasn't until the instant before she slammed the door to her room that Elizabeth thought she heard a faint reply.

"We'll see about that."

Bantam Books in the Sweet Valley High Series
Ask your bookseller for the books you have missed

SWEET VALLEY HIGH

POWER PLAY

Written by
Kate William

Created by
FRANCINE PASCAL

BANTAM BOOKS
TORONTO • NEW YORK • LONDON • SYDNEY • AUCKLAND

RL 4, IL age 12 and up

POWER PLAY
A Bantam Book / January 1984
14 printings through January 1987

Sweet Valley High is a trademark of Francine Pascal

Conceived by Francine Pascal

Produced by Cloverdale Press, Inc.

Cover art by James Mathewuse

ISBN 0-553-26746-9

Published simultaneously in the United States and Canada

Bantam Books are published by Bantam Books, Inc. Its trademark, consisting
of the words "Bantam Books" and the portrayal of a rooster, is Registered in
U.S. Patent and Trademark Office and in other countries. Marca Registrada.
Bantam Books, Inc., 666 Fifth Avenue, New York, New York 10103.

PRINTED IN THE UNITED STATES OF AMERICA

O   23 22 21 20 19 18 17 16 15

POWER
PLAY

One

Elizabeth Wakefield didn't know how messy things would get with Robin Wilson and the sorority pledging, until she was in too deep to back out.

It happened, as so many things seemed to, because of Jessica, her twin sister, who had just been elected president of Pi Beta Alpha, the snobbiest sorority at Sweet Valley High. Elizabeth was a member, too, but she hardly ever went to meetings. She didn't like the club's style and was too busy writing the "Eyes and Ears" column for the school paper to give the members much of her time.

"Eyes and Ears" was a regular feature, filled with hot, fun items about the students at Sweet Valley High. Sources remained anonymous. Even the identity of the writer herself had at first been a secret, though by now everyone knew it was Elizabeth.

The column was always humorous and light. Elizabeth had been very careful to stay away from any topic that could be mean or hurtful, even before anyone knew who was writing the column. Mr. Collins, the faculty adviser, had warned her early on about the dangers of anonymous power. It was advice Elizabeth would recall when she confronted another kind of anonymous power—one that threatened to tear Robin Wilson and the Pi Betas apart.

Robin believed herself to be Jessica's best friend, which was, at best, a dangerous assumption. Elizabeth became acutely aware of the fact one day when the phone in the kitchen rang and it was Robin Wilson's mother trying to locate her daughter.

"Gee, Mrs. Wilson, I haven't seen her."

"Is this Elizabeth? I think Robin is on her way over there with some things she's delivering for your sister."

"Oh," said Elizabeth, frowning. It was just like Jessica to use Robin as a messenger.

"If she shows up, ask her to call home, will you, dear?"

"Of course, Mrs. Wilson," Elizabeth said.

And then, silence. Although the conversation seemed to be over, Mrs. Wilson didn't hang up. Elizabeth could almost hear her on the other end of the line, making up her mind to say more.

"Elizabeth," Mrs. Wilson said at last, "can I ask you something? Does Robin seem—unhappy to you? I know that having you and Jessica as friends is the best thing that's happened to her since we moved to Sweet Valley. But—"

Elizabeth thought for a moment. "Well, I don't know. She seems all right to me," she said, at a loss for a better answer.

And then Elizabeth was totally astounded to hear Mrs. Wilson crying. "Oh, Elizabeth, you've got to help Robin! She's going to drop out of school!"

"What?"

"Yes! Even though she doesn't show it, she's so miserable. She's a little overweight, you know, and she thinks she's very unpopular." Mrs. Wilson took a deep breath, and when she spoke again, her voice was steadier. "Elizabeth, I know it's none of my business, but is Robin going to be asked to pledge your sorority? It would mean so much to her."

"We've gotten behind on nominations," Elizabeth said, "because the old president moved away. But now Jessica is president, and she told me that she's going to put Robin's name up at the next meeting."

"Yes, I know," Mrs. Wilson said and sighed. "But . . ."

"But what, Mrs. Wilson?"

"Well, Jessica is so busy, she might never get around to it. This is silly of me. Never mind, Elizabeth. Ask Robin to call home, will you? And, please, don't mention this to her. She'd be mortified."

Elizabeth hung up the phone. The conversation, however, continued to replay itself in her mind. Robin Wilson drop out of school? Why, she was one of the smartest girls at Sweet Valley! True, she was "a little overweight," as her mother had said. Much more than a little, actually. But she always seemed so cheerful and friendly.

Just then the phone rang again. It was her twin.

"Jessica Wakefield, you were supposed to be home an hour ago to help me clean the house, and you know it!" Elizabeth's anger came through loud and clear.

After listening to Jessica's breezy excuses for a moment or two, Elizabeth impatiently cut in. "You always have *very*, *very* important things to do when work is involved. What is it this time? You have to pick up your cleaning? What else?"

Again she listened, but this time an amused smile crept over her face. "*You* are picking up books at the library?" She was surprised her sister even knew her way there.

"OK, Jess, get here as soon as you can. Mom said the house had to be absolutely squeaky clean for her dinner party tonight."

Before Jessica could object, Elizabeth hung up, cutting her sister off in the middle of a sentence. Whenever Jessica talked that fast, Elizabeth knew she was up to something. Resisting the temptation to guess what the "something" was this time, she walked into the living room, trying to decide between vacuuming and dusting.

Elizabeth's usual sense of humor, momentarily out to lunch, returned in full force as she remembered her sister's last attempt to get out of serious work.

"Let's share the work," Jessica had said. "You clean the johns, and I'll arrange the flowers."

Alone in the living room, Elizabeth laughed out loud. One thing about Jessica—you had to give her credit for sheer nerve.

Elizabeth was plugging in the vacuum cleaner

when the doorbell rang. She opened the door to find Robin Wilson, loaded down with books and dry cleaner's bags.

"Hi, Elizabeth, is Jessica home?" she asked shyly.

"What makes you think I'm not Jessica?" Elizabeth responded with friendly playfulness.

Looking awkward and uncomfortable, Robin blushed. "I don't mean to offend you, Liz, really I don't, but I'm pretty sure Jessica's never dressed like that in her life."

Elizabeth looked down at her favorite old jeans and flannel shirt and started to chuckle. "You're right, Robin. Come on in. Jess should be home pretty soon."

Robin plopped down on the sofa, rummaged around in her purse for something, and finally came up with a large chocolate bar. She unwrapped it and hungrily started munching.

"You're really lucky, Liz, having a terrific sister like Jessica." The chocolate bar was disappearing fast.

"That's me, all right, lucky Liz," she replied dryly, hypnotized by Robin's rhythmic chewing.

"Robin, doesn't eating like that make you"— *don't say "fat,"* she warned herself—"break out?"

"Oh, no," said Robin, licking her sticky fingers. "I never get zits, just pounds. But I just wasn't meant to be slim like you and Jessica. It's got something to do with my bones—or is it my metabolism? Anyway, it's just my sad fate."

Elizabeth looked at Robin dubiously. She was convinced Robin's heaviness was due to the way she ate—especially if this was typical.

Though Elizabeth and Jessica certainly didn't have Robin's figure problems, they still watched their diets carefully. Slim, five foot six, the sisters were both beautiful: shoulder-length, sun-streaked blond hair, flashing blue-green eyes, and perfect skin. Elizabeth was four minutes older, but they were identical right down to the tiny dimple each had in her left cheek. Although they wore the same size clothes, they never dressed alike, except for identical lavalieres that they wore on gold chains around their necks. The lavalieres had been presents from their parents on the twins' sixteenth birthday.

The only way a stranger could tell them apart was that Elizabeth had a tiny beauty mark on her right shoulder. Their friends might notice that only Elizabeth wore a wristwatch. It was a telling detail. Time was never a problem for Jessica. She always felt that things didn't really start until she got there, anyway. And if she happened to be a little late—let 'em wait.

That "let 'em wait" attitude was what Elizabeth was inwardly fuming about.

"Look, Robin, Jessica may have gotten held

up somewhere, so maybe you could call her later or—"

"That's all right, Liz," Robin said, struggling to get out of the deep cushions. "I just wanted to drop off her cleaning and the books she wanted from the library."

Cleaning? Books? *Bingo!* Elizabeth exclaimed to herself. Jessica was definitely up to something.

"Why in the world are you doing Jessica's errands, Robin?"

"Well, she said she had something *very, very* important to do. Besides, that's what best friends are for—to do favors for each other."

Oh, Robin, Elizabeth thought, *if you're Jessica's best friend, Attila the Hun is the prom King.* Elizabeth knew that doing favors was a one-way street with her sister. Jessica always let people do favors for her. It was her way of being kind to the "little people."

"I'll get out of your way, Liz," Robin was saying. "There's just one thing, and I probably shouldn't even mention it."

"Let me guess. Jessica forgot to pay for the cleaning."

"Oh, no, that doesn't matter. It's about—well, it's about Pi Beta Alpha."

"What about PBA, Robin?"

Robin blushed. "It's just that I thought—I mean I know—that Jessica is waiting for the right time to put my name up for membership. I *know* she wants me to be a PBA, but she's always so busy with really important things, and maybe she's forgotten this is my last chance to pledge. I can't pledge as a senior, so it's either now or never, Liz. I don't know what to do. It means everything to me." Robin looked as though she might burst into tears at any moment.

Don't cry, Elizabeth thought. *Oh, Robin, please don't cry.* Belonging to a group whose main activities were putting on lip gloss and talking about boys was definitely not worth crying about.

"Robin, I'm sure it will all work out," she blurted, realizing as she spoke that she sounded just the way her mother did when things were definitely *not* going to work out.

Robin brightened at this. "You think so, Liz? I mean, I do think I know why Jessica hasn't put my name up. I bet she thinks it would be pushy—not really fair, you know, to nominate her best friend."

Elizabeth stared at Robin, completely amazed at how blind she was to Jessica's true character. Her twin was many things. A great dancer, a terrific cheerleader, a sensational surfer—but fair? Jessica could turn on the devastating charm when she wanted something, but going out of her way to do the "right" thing or to be "fair" just wasn't her style.

"Robin, is PBA so important to you?"

"Oh, yes, Liz, it is! I was just thinking—maybe you could remind Jessica?"

Elizabeth studied Robin Wilson's pleading face. It would do no good to "remind" Jessica, Elizabeth knew. Because her sister had told Elizabeth over and over again that Robin definitely did *not* fit the picture of the typical slim and pretty Pi Beta. Jessica would never nominate Robin, no matter how many times she might have promised. Yet Robin was a really nice girl, Elizabeth thought, and certainly smarter than most of the sorority members. PBA could use a new image—even if its members didn't think so.

"Robin, there's a meeting the day after tomorrow. Instead of reminding Jessica, why don't *I* put your name up?"

"*You*, Liz? You'd do that for me?"

Elizabeth laughed. "Sure. But, Robin, please don't think PBA is the answer to every—"

"Liz, you're wonderful, every bit as wonderful as your sister!" Robin interrupted, clearly in a world of her own. "Can I use your phone to call my mother? She'll be so excited. Maybe she'll even take me shopping this afternoon. The kids in PBA have such great clothes—I'd just die if I embarrassed them."

The rush of words continued, but Elizabeth

tuned it out while showing Robin to the wall phone in the kitchen.

I did the right thing, she told herself as she walked back into the living room. *Why should Robin be kept out of PBA because she's a little overweight? All right, a lot overweight.* She heaved a sigh. She knew her sister would be upset. In fact, Elizabeth was sure Jessica would fly into one of her four-color, full-stereo rages.

Where *was* Jessica anyway? Probably at the mall with Lila Fowler. From Elizabeth's viewpoint that kind of afternoon would be as much fun as a month in the dentist's chair. Lila was the daughter of the wealthiest man in Sweet Valley, George Fowler, and both daughter and father were the town's biggest snobs. They lived in an elegant mansion in the expensive hill section of Sweet Valley. Jessica was forever envious of the Fowlers' money and house—that is, when she wasn't being envious of the money and house Bruce Patman's family had. Elizabeth thought that the feud between the old-money Patmans and the new-money Fowlers was really very silly, but not Jessica. New or old, money was never silly to her.

Elizabeth preferred their split-level house in the valley. Actually, she thought everything about Sweet Valley was terrific, especially the gently rolling hills, the quaint downtown area, and the beach, which was only fifteen minutes from their house.

Robin burst back into the room, all aflutter. "My mom is soooooo excited!" She always told me that being best friends with the Wakefield twins could be great for me," she gushed. Searching through her bag, she found another candy bar and began unwrapping it.

Elizabeth sighed inwardly. *Now what have I done?*

Robin was suddenly hugging and kissing her in an explosion of enthusiasm and happiness. It was too much for Elizabeth, who laughed and returned the hug, thinking that if the prospect of joining the Pi Betas could make someone so happy, she just might ask the whole junior class to pledge.

Letting go of Elizabeth, Robin held out her chocolate bar. "You want a bite?" she offered.

"No, thanks, Robin."

Robin Wilson stood there beaming, her eyes filled with happiness. "If there's nothing I can do for you, I think I'll hurry home. Mom's taking me shopping."

"Robin, you really don't have to—"

But Robin was already at the door. She yanked it open, almost toppling Jessica, who was just about to walk in.

"Jessica!" Robin shrieked. Elizabeth watched

her sister shrink in distaste as the ecstatic Robin reached out to hug her.

"Hi, Robin." Jessica's total lack of enthusiasm was painfully obvious—but not to Robin.

"Omigod, Jessica, I'm soooo excited! Your sister is as wonderful as you are! Mom's taking me shopping! Got to go!"

And Robin bounced away, leaving Jessica standing there flabbergasted.

"What in the world was that?"

Elizabeth broke into helpless laughter.

"Why was that fat wimp pawing at me and gushing all over the place?" Jessica demanded.

"I'll tell you, Jess. But first, you tell me where you've been. And don't tell me you were out getting books and picking up the dry cleaning, since your best friend Robin Wilson did that for you."

"My best friend?"

"*She* thinks so."

"Well, she's all right, sometimes. It *is* nice to have someone to help you out."

"Run errands for you. Lick your boots."

"Liz Wakefield, you know perfectly well I only use leather cream on my boots."

It was pure Jessica. Elizabeth was the writer, but when Jessica needed to wiggle out of an unpleasant conversation, she had quite a way

13

with words. But Elizabeth wasn't letting her get away with it—not this time.

"Where were you that you couldn't help clean the house? And where'd you get that new bit of loot?"

Jessica acted mystified. "You mean this?" She touched the lovely sapphire-blue silk scarf knotted around her neck.

"Yes, *this*. Where did you get it?"

"Lila Fowler gave it to me."

"You were with Lila again. Is that what was so important?"

"Lila Fowler happens to be the class act of Sweet Valley High, Liz, and you know it. Her aunt sent her the scarf from New York, but Lila said it isn't her best color, so she gave it to me."

Elizabeth shook her head in wonder. The scarf was really beautiful, and obviously quite expensive. *Do the rich always share the wealth like this?* she wondered.

She looked at Jessica, standing there smiling from ear to ear.

"Jess, I don't begrudge you a new scarf, but I don't appreciate being left here alone to do all the cleaning. Not to mention entertaining *your* best friend."

Jessica rolled her beautiful eyes heavenward. "Robin can get carried away four hundred and thirty-seven times a day, you know? What was she babbling about, anyway?"

"Oh, nothing much, really. Apparently you're so busy all the time you don't remember how much Robin wants to pledge Pi Beta."

"Oh, that." Jessica sighed. "I keep forgetting."

"Uh-huh. And this is her last chance."

"It is?" Innocence and Jessica Wakefield were one and the same.

"So," Elizabeth pushed on, "knowing you were going to put her up sooner or later anyway, *I* promised to sponsor her for membership at the next meeting."

Jessica's mouth dropped open. "You promised her *what*? Are you crazy?"

Now Elizabeth was all innocence. You don't live with Jessica Wakefield for sixteen years without learning something.

"Gee, Jess, what do you mean?"

"That—that tub of lard in Pi Beta Alpha?"

"But, Jess," Elizabeth said slyly, "she's your best friend. She told me so."

"That has nothing to do with it. There's a problem of—image."

But Elizabeth was not about to be out-maneuvered. "Image? That doesn't seem to bother you when she carries your books and cleaning for you."

"I like to be kind to everybody, Elizabeth,"

15

Jessica cooed. "You know that. But pledging Pi Beta? Well, look—you know Robin's only interested in studying. She's taking about thirty-seven extra courses. I'm just not sure PBA is right for her."

Anyone who didn't know Jessica as well as Elizabeth did would have been totally convinced that Robin's welfare was her first and only concern.

But Elizabeth wasn't buying. "Well, I think it is," she said calmly. "I've never seen anyone as happy as Robin was when I told her I'd sponsor her."

If Elizabeth was calm, Jessica was anything but. By now she had given up even trying to appear reasonable. She was beside herself with rage and frustration.

"Boy, now I have *really* seen everything!" she wailed. "How can my own sister—my identical twin, no less—be so totally, hopelessly *idiotic*?"

Elizabeth let out a breath. "I gather I've done something wrong."

"*That* is the understatement of the week," Jessica agreed sarcastically. "Robin Wilson in the Pi Betas? With *us*? With Lila Fowler? One look at that shape and they'll be calling us the Pi *Butterball* Alphas! Oh, really, Liz, are you completely absent from this universe?"

"It's only a silly sorority," Elizabeth reasoned.

"Only a—" This was too much. Jessica was speechless.

Elizabeth sighed. "Jessica, for heaven's sake, don't come unglued. I've promised, and that's that. Robin Wilson's going to be a Pi Beta."

"Oh, is she?"

What was going on here? Elizabeth looked searchingly at Jessica for some answer, but Jessica wouldn't meet her eyes.

"Look," Elizabeth said at last, "if I sponsor Robin and you're the president of Pi Beta Alpha—*and* her best friend—she's in."

Jessica's only response was to toss her head and stomp out of the room and up the stairs. It wasn't until the instant before she slammed the door to her room that Elizabeth thought she heard a faint reply.

"We'll see about that."

Two

"The meeting will now come to order."

Jessica looked around the room at the members of PBA—chatting, checking their faces in compact mirrors, brushing their hair, and, in general, not paying attention to her. If there was one thing Jessica couldn't bear, it was people *not* paying attention to her.

In her best snap-to-it-or-else voice, she repeated, "The meeting will *now* come to order!"

Noting that her sister wasn't there yet, Jessica decided to have the shortest meeting in PBA history and avoid the problem of Robin Wilson.

"I know there isn't any old business, and

nobody took minutes at the last meeting, so there isn't anything to be read. And everybody knows we have thirty-seven dollars and fifty cents in the treasury, so there's no need for a treasurer's report. Sooooo, if no one has any new business, we can—"

"Did I hear someone mention new business?" interrupted a slightly out of breath Elizabeth, coming into the room. "Sorry to be late. I got hung up at the newspaper office."

Everyone but Jessica was surprised to see Elizabeth at a meeting. It had been ages. The other members knew that PBA wasn't crucial to Elizabeth, but most of them didn't resent her. She was smart, a big deal on the paper, and generally good for the PBA image. She was also, of course, the president's twin sister.

And speaking of the president, she seemed very anxious to end the meeting.

"Liz, you are very late, and we are almost ready to adjourn," Jessica began stiffly.

"But didn't I just hear you call for new business?" Elizabeth said sweetly, shooting her twin a warning look that clearly said, *Don't even try it.*

Jessica got the message. "Well, if you have something totally and absolutely important to bring up, I guess you can," she said reluctantly.

Elizabeth turned to the group. "I do have

something important to bring up. I would like to nominate someone for membership in Pi Beta Alpha, someone who is a friend of mine and a *good* friend of my sister's—Robin Wilson."

Total silence greeted Elizabeth's announcement. And then—pandemonium.

"Robin Wilson—one of *us*?"

"She's that—pudgy one, isn't she?"

"Liz put her name up, so she must think it's OK."

"You sure she's not kidding?"

Tight-lipped and stormy-eyed, Jessica let the stream of chatter go on for a few more minutes, then called the meeting to order again.

"Is there anyone who objects to Robin Wilson being nominated for Pi Beta Alpha?" she asked. The answer was a foregone conclusion. No one dared to object to a friend of the Wakefield twins. And Jessica didn't dare say how she really felt. For one thing, Elizabeth would blast her. And if Robin ever found out, that would mark the end of her days as Jessica's handmaiden.

After the meeting broke up, Jessica, sparks flying from her blue-green eyes, walked over to her sister. "Are you proud of yourself now, Little Miss Do-a-Good-Deed-Every-Day?"

Elizabeth cringed at the anger in her sister's voice.

"Look, Jess, it's not the end of the world. She'll be a terrific addition to PBA!"

"Prove it!" Jessica snapped.

"Robin is nice, she's sweet, and she's very smart."

"And she's surrounded by two tons of fat!"

"Two tons, Jess?" Elizabeth smiled in spite of herself. "Really, how could a girl as nice as Robin possibly hurt the grand and glorious image of PBA?"

Jessica's eyes narrowed in suspicion. "You're being sarcastic, aren't you? It's really a very unattractive trait, Elizabeth. And if I were you, I wouldn't get too smug too soon."

This time it was Elizabeth's turn to be suspicious. "Just what is that crack supposed to mean, Jessica?"

"Oh, nothing at all, sister dear," said Jessica airily. "You do remember, don't you, that Pi Beta Alpha pledges have to perform certain—uh, tasks before they can be voted on for full membership?"

"Jessica Wakefield, I'm warning you."

"Liz, I'm truly hurt that you would think I would do anything sneaky. You really *must* put a leash on that suspicious mind of yours. I just meant that I'll do everything *I* can to make sure Robin has a fair chance to prove herself worthy of Pi Beta Alpha. Sooooo—Lila Fowler, Cara

Walker, and I will guide Robin through her pledge period."

"Lucky Robin," Elizabeth muttered.

"Somebody has to give Robin the good news. The three of us are going over to see her now. Do you want to come?"

Elizabeth shook her head. "I have to meet Todd in a few minutes. Too bad, I'd love to be there when she gets the official word. She's going to do cartwheels!"

"*Fat* chance." Jessica sneered. Then, seeing the look of disapproval on Elizabeth's face she quickly added, "I won't hurt her feelings. You know it's not in my nature to be nasty—even to a wimp like Robin."

"Yes, Jess, you're famous for that. You're the world's heavyweight champ of kindness."

"Heavyweight—how appropriate!" Jessica retorted, breezing past Elizabeth and out the door.

A half-hour later the three girls were ringing the Wilson doorbell.

"I don't think anyone's home, Jess."

"Don't be silly, Cara," Jessica snapped. "Where else would she be?"

Just then Robin opened the door, practically

ripping it off its hinges in her excitement. "Jessica! And Lila and Cara—what a surprise!"

Jessica was full of the dignity of her office. "May we come in, Robin? We have something totally serious and vital to tell you."

"Sure, sure, Jessica, come on in. This is so terrific—having you here and all. . . . Can I get you something? A soda maybe—or I could fix chocolate shakes? We've got some really great éclairs. Or how about some ice cream sandwiches?" Robin's steady stream of nervous chatter visibly annoyed Jessica and made Cara and Lila yawn.

What's the matter with me? thought Robin, finally slowing down enough to notice their reactions. *Why do I always say the wrong things around people I want to impress?*

"Oh, gee, I'm sorry," she said aloud. "You don't have time to listen to me babble on and on about food."

Assuming her best president-of-the-sorority pose, Jessica announced, "Robin, you are fortunate enough to have had your name put up for membership in Pi Beta Alpha. You are now officially a pledge."

The smile of pure happiness on Robin's face was so heartbreakingly sincere and grateful that it almost made Jessica change her plans. Almost, but not quite.

"Oh, Jessica, thank you! And you, too, Lila and Cara! This is so super I can hardly believe it's happening to me! When do I start? What do I do?"

Frowning, Jessica tried to hose down Robin's burning enthusiasm. "You know, Robin, being a member of PBA isn't just wearing a special jacket and spending time with all the best people in school, or even being in on all the really important things that happen in Sweet Valley."

A slightly subdued Robin vigorously nodded understanding.

"As a pledge," Jessica continued, "you have to do certain things—things that prove you are worthy of being a Pi Beta. You have to prove your loyalty to us."

"I'll always be loyal to Pi Beta Alpha," Robin swore. "All my life!"

"That's easy to say, Robin," Cara interjected disdainfully.

"She's right, Robin," said Jessica. "Some of the things you will be asked to do may be a little difficult for you."

"Nothing would be too hard, Jessica, nothing in the whole world. No matter what it is, I'll do it," Robin vowed.

It was like taking candy from a baby. Jessica plunged on.

"OK. Tomorrow. Right after school. Girls' gym. Don't be late!"

As the three sorority girls got up to leave, Lila whispered to Jessica, "What a drab little existence. Let's get out of here before she offers us another éclair!"

An ecstatic Robin closed the door and headed straight for the kitchen. Pulling a whole cherry cheesecake from the refrigerator, she began eating to calm her nerves. At last! She, Robin Wilson, was actually going to be a Pi Beta Alpha. She was going to be popular. All she had to do was get through pledging. How hard could that be?

"Tell me everything, Jess. How did Robin take the news?" Elizabeth dropped her books on a table and descended on her sister. Jessica was wearing leotards and exercising with Jane Fonda via video cassette.

"Do you think my thighs look all right, Liz?" Jessica asked worriedly, flipping the TV off and throwing a towel around her neck. She decided to do fifty extra leg lifts, just in case.

"You thighs are not important right now. What happened with Robin?"

"Thighs are *always* important. Anyway, Robin took the news with disgusting offers of food and undying loyalty. I really think that girl wants us all to be as fat as she is."

"Jessica!"

"OK, OK. The wimp is happy. Does that make you happy? Do you *mind* if I finish exercising?"

"Not at all." Elizabeth peered at her sister. "Where did you get all that gold, Jess?"

"Gold? What gold?" Jessica wiped her face off with the towel.

"Those earrings you're wearing—they cost ten times more than your allowance, which I know you just spent on albums."

Jessica placed protective fingers over the small, delicate earrings. "These? Don't be silly. I didn't buy them. Lila's aunt sent them to her, and she didn't really like them, soooo—they're mine. Aren't they great?"

"Yeah, great." Elizabeth started up the stairs, then paused. "Don't you think it's kind of odd for Lila to be so generous all of a sudden?"

"Don't get all upset, sister dear. There's nothing wrong in accepting a few gifts from a good friend."

"Maybe not. Well, I have a history paper to finish." She started up the stairs again.

"By the way, Liz," Jessica said casually, "something rather interesting is going to happen tomorrow."

"What are you up to now, Jess?"

"Nothing—nothing at all, but I suggest you be at the track right after school."

Elizabeth dashed up to her locker the next afternoon just as Todd Wilkins, her boyfriend, strolled up to his.

"Hurry, Todd. I don't want to be late."

"Hurry? Late? School's out. Time to relax." He grabbed her by the waist and pulled her into his arms. "And I have the perfect way to relax you."

Elizabeth melted against him, happily allowing his lips to caress hers.

"Liz," Todd murmured, "let's go for a walk right now. I want to be alone with you."

"Oh, Todd, I can't," she said, remembering Jessica's comment about "something interesting" happening. "I think I've got trouble. Big trouble."

Slipping a finger under her chin, Todd lifted Elizabeth's face to his and saw that there was worry in her eyes. She needed cheering up, he decided.

"Don't tell me. Let me gaze into zee future." He curved his hands around an imaginary crystal ball. "Ziss beeg trouble starts with a *J* and look almost as bee-yoo-tiful as you."

"Be serious, you idiot. And don't start in on

my sister. Jessica is only part of the problem." A long sigh. "OK, Jessica *is* the problem. I don't have time to explain, but we've got to get over to the track—now! She tugged him along the hall and through the big center doors out onto the lawn.

"Just give me a clue!" Todd panted, running to keep up with her. "What's Jessica up to that has you so worried?"

"I don't know. That's what has me so worried. Hurry, Todd!"

"I'm hurrying, I'm hurrying! Hey, what's all that noise coming from the track?"

They broke into a sprint, reaching the track just in time to see a sweating, gasping Robin Wilson stumble past.

"What in the world—?" Elizabeth gasped.

The stands were partly filled with students, some cheering, but most just curiously watching Robin lumber her way around the track.

"Way to go, Robin!"

"Don't fall down, Wilson. You'll dent the track!"

Elizabeth whirled around at this remark, intending to shut up the jerk who'd made it—and spotted Bruce Patman lounging against his black Porsche, a sneer on his good-looking face.

"Be quiet, you moron!" she snapped. She turned back to Todd. "I am just about ready to commit murder!" she said. Then she made her way over to Lila and Cara. "How could you two do this to Robin—to anyone?"

"Hi, Liz, welcome to the Olympics for chubbos!" a familiar voice shouted from behind.

This sent Lila, Cara, Bruce, and others who were close enough to hear into fits of wild laughter.

"Jessica Wakefield, this is unbelievable!" Elizabeth fumed. Jessica was sitting off to the side, busily ignoring Bruce's presence, for she had recently broken up with him. Bruce's incredible egotism had almost turned Jessica into his servant. When she'd caught him with another girl, Jessica had unleashed her matchless fury.

She didn't answer Elizabeth.

"Don't you think dear Robin looks *très chic* in her gray sweat shorts and tank top?" Lila contributed. "So perfect for that round body, *n'est-ce pas?*" The group laughed again.

Elizabeth was furious. "You three are—are—well, you know what you are!" She stomped off toward the totally exhausted Robin, who was leaning against a fence.

Elizabeth had gone only a few steps when Jessica's voice reached her. "Maybe if she ran around the track about a hundred and thirty-seven times a day for the next five years, she might lose some of that fat!"

Elizabeth reached Robin just as PBA's newest pledge was almost able to breathe again.

"Robin, are you all right? You look terrible!"

"I've never looked good in shorts, Liz."

"No, no, Robin, I just meant that you look so tired. Why in the world did you do it?"

Astonishment was written all over Robin's sweaty, round face, "Why? Elizabeth, it's one of the things a pledge *has* to do to prove her loyalty to Pi Beta Alpha. You certainly should understand that. Besides, it isn't that bad. I only have to jog around the track five times a day for just *one* week."

"A week? Robin, you don't have to do this. Joining PBA, or any sorority, isn't that important, believe me."

"Not that *important*?" Robin drew herself up to her full height. "It's everything to me, Liz. And I can do it. I will do anything to be a Pi Beta!"

Elizabeth was waiting in the girls' locker room as Robin came in from her last day of jogging.

"Robin, you are a real inspiration," Elizabeth admitted. "I think you're just terrific!"

"Thanks," Robin said dully.

Thanks? Where was the happy smile? The sense of purpose? The cheery enthusiasm?

"You should be really happy, Robin. What could be harder than what you went through this week?"

"Saturday."

"Saturday?"

Big, brown, tearful eyes looked up at Elizabeth. "Jogging was hard, Liz, but I did it. I don't know if I can handle Saturday."

Elizabeth was almost too afraid to ask. "What's happening Saturday, Robin?"

The tears were spilling over by this time.

"Robin, please tell me."

Through sobs, Robin got out, "I have to go to the beach!"

"The beach? You're worried about the beach, Robin? Why? You're a good swimmer—I've seen you. It'll be easy!" Elizabeth let out a sigh of relief. "You had me worried for a minute. I thought maybe you had to climb Mount Everest."

"I could have done that, Liz. I just don't know how I can show up at the beach on Saturday in—in a bikini! And play volleyball!"

Oh, boy, Elizabeth thought, *we have a problem*.

"Do you have a bikini, Robin?" she asked gently.

"Kind of."

"A kind of bikini?"

Turning away in embarrassment, Robin muttered, "Well, it's a two-piece suit that's too small, so it looks like a bikini, kind of."

Elizabeth looked down at the tiled floor thoughtfully, then made a quick decision. "You know something, Robin? Todd and I and Enid and her boyfriend, George, are going to the beach on Saturday. We always play volleyball. You can be on our team, OK?"

"Really?" The look of thanks on Robin's tear-stained face was almost too much for Elizabeth to bear.

"Really. We'll pick you up."

"Maybe it'll rain."

"It won't rain, Robin. We'll have a good time." *And*, thought Elizabeth, *so will three witches I know.*

Saturday was sunny and beautiful, as it almost always was in Sweet Valley. Elizabeth knew it was going to be a difficult day for Robin—and for her.

When Todd arrived, she greeted him with a special smile and a hug. It was wonderful to be able to spend her free days with him. Quickly she jumped into the car and explained the circumstances.

"You'll help?" Elizabeth asked, already knowing the answer.

"I'll help. Did you ever doubt it?" Todd kissed her nose lightly, then started the car.

Robin, self-conscious and red-faced, took off her terry tent robe, revealing a very tight two-piece suit to the amused looks of the usual Saturday beach crowd.

Robin hung in through the almost endless day, bolstered by Elizabeth, Todd, Enid, and George. Whenever possible, they encouraged her to laugh and always accompanied her into the water.

The volleyball game proved to be the toughest part of Robin's day. Bruce Patman, egged on by Lila and Cara, took obvious delight in shooting one ball after another right at Robin. Jessica didn't join in in encouraging Bruce, but she did send a few impossible shots in Robin's direction.

"Way to go, Wilson," Bruce jeered. "Anyone into blubber would call your moves awesome."

Somehow though, with a little help, Robin made it through the day. "You were right, Liz!" she said when most of the crowd had gone home. "I *can* do it!"

"I knew you could, Robin." Elizabeth looked around. "Well, all packed up. I guess we'll drop you off first, Robin."

"Oh, I don't need a ride home, Liz. Thanks anyway, but Jessica and Lila offered me a ride."

Wonderful, Elizabeth thought. *Just what you need.*

"I'm really impressed with you, Robin. We all are."

Praise from Jessica Wakefield? Robin was speechless.

"You've done everything we asked you to do. You've done—pretty well."

"Pretty well" from Jessica was like a standing ovation from anybody else. Robin was ecstatic. She jumped up and tried to hug Jessica.

"Wait, Robin," Jessica said, stepping out of range. "There's just *one* more thing you have to do to prove your loyalty to PBA."

"Anything, Jessica. Anything!"

"You have to get Bruce Patman to take you to the Discomarathon next Saturday night."

Three

Elizabeth was on her way out the door of Sweet Valley High when she saw a forlorn figure sitting under a tree. It was Robin Wilson, hunched over, tightly hugging her knees to her chest, her books strewn carelessly on the grass.

Moving closer, Elizabeth saw a look of utter despair on Robin's face. Why wasn't she feeling better about herself? Elizabeth wondered. She had met all the challenges that Jessica, Lila, and Cara had thrown her way. She'd practically been Wonder Woman. They hadn't gotten the better of her for one moment. *Not yet, anyway*, Elizabeth thought, suddenly feeling a twinge of anxiety.

Robin Wilson was proving to be a first-class candidate for Pi Beta Alpha, if determination and grit meant anything. But Elizabeth couldn't escape the persistent feeling of guilt over nominating Robin for PBA. Maybe it had been a big mistake, she kept thinking. Jessica and Lila and the others could ruin Robin if this kept up.

"How goes it, Pledge Wilson?" Elizabeth asked cheerfully.

Robin looked up, her eyes brimming with tears. Her chin began to quiver uncontrollably.

"Robin, please don't," Elizabeth begged, but Robin couldn't help herself. Tears spilled from her eyes, rolling down her cheeks in unending streams.

"Omigod, Elizabeth," Robin wailed. "It's hopeless!"

"What are you talking about, Robin? What's hopeless?"

"I'll never make PBA now."

Elizabeth sighed with relief. Was that all? "Sure, you will. Everybody's amazed at what you've done."

Robin sniffled. "You think so?"

"Absolutely. I wouldn't have put you up for membership if I didn't think—"

"I never thought they'd make me do so many really hard things!" Robin cried out in a mixture of anger and desperation. "Nobody else ever had to."

Oh, how I'd like to get even with those snobs! Elizabeth thought.

"Well, Robin," she said, "it's probably because they know you can handle it."

"I have, haven't I?" said Robin, and she sounded surprised at the determination in her voice. "I sure have."

Elizabeth was relieved to see Robin showing some pride in herself.

"But now they've really finished me, Liz!" Robin moaned. "Sometimes I think they're just tormenting me. That they'll never let me be a Pi Beta Alpha."

"Who put you up for membership, Robin? I did. Elizabeth Wakefield! Do you think I would ever be involved with anything like that?"

Robin paused and looked away. "I don't know."

"Well, *I* know. And I'm here to help you. Don't you worry. You'll be a Pi Beta if I have anything to say. That's a promise!"

"But, Liz—they say I have to get—to get— omigod—I have to get Bruce Patman to take me to the Discomarathon next Saturday night!"

"Who?" *Please, let me have heard her wrong,* Elizabeth prayed. *Anyone but him!*

"Bruce Patman!"

Elizabeth's heart sank.

"I might as well ask Elvis Presley!"

"Robin," Elizabeth reminded her gently, "Elvis has been dead for—"

"That's just my point. I'd have a better chance with a dead superstar than a live Bruce Patman!"

How could they do such a thing? Elizabeth fumed. And before she knew what she was doing, the words were out.

"Robin, you go on and ask him. I *know* he'll say yes."

"What?"

You've gone off the edge, Lizzie, Elizabeth was thinking.

"Liz, are you feeling all right?"

"Bruce Patman should be honored to go to the dance with you, Robin. One of the smartest girls in Sweet Valley! One of the nicest—"

Robin was watching her now, anxiously.

"—and one of the warmest."

Robin looked down again. "Thanks, Liz. Nice try. But guys like Bruce don't care about those things. Me—ask Bruce Patman? No way."

"Promise you'll ask him."

"Positive thinking is one thing, Liz, but that's a fantasy!"

"Promise!"

"Oh, all right. But he'll never—"

"Robin."

38

"But he couldn't—"

"Robin!"

Robin shrugged in resignation. *"Fantasy Island, here I come!"*

She rose slowly and gathered her books. Trying to smooth out the wrinkles in her dark red tent dress, she shuffled off across the lawn, her head hanging.

Elizabeth watched her, wondering how even Jessica could have asked such a thing of Robin. She also wondered how she, Elizabeth, could have practically promised Robin that Bruce would take her.

It was Robin's sad face that had thrown her. *But now what do I do?* Elizabeth agonized. And why should she have to do anything? *Because you put Robin up, that's why. You got her into this mess.*

"Oh, all right," she muttered out loud. "But how can I possibly get Bruce Patman to—"

Speak of the devil. There he was right now, across the campus on the tennis court, thwacking a yellow ball with powerful, precise strokes. Bruce Patman prided himself on three things: his black Porsche, his good looks, and his tennis.

Which one, Elizabeth wondered, was his greatest weakness?

Sliding nimbly across the court in his designer tennis shorts, Bruce slammed a beautiful cross-court shot past the luckless freshman who was trying out for the Sweet Valley varsity team.

"Tough." Bruce laughed smugly.

"Some shot," said an admiring voice.

When Bruce gazed into the sun, there stood lovely Jessica Wakefield. *Well, well,* he thought. *Maybe Jessica wants another chance with me.*

"Helping some fortunate freshman *not* make the team, I see," said the beautiful Wakefield twin, and Bruce knew at once that it wasn't Jessica.

"Hi, Liz." He glanced at the freshman, who was chasing down the ball that had whistled past him into the far corner. "Too bad," Bruce said. "Looks like he hasn't got what it takes."

He strolled up to the wire fence around the court, brushing back his dark hair as he walked. "So, Liz. How's the newspaper going?"

"OK."

"Say, when is *The Oracle* going to do a decent story on the star of the varsity tennis team?"

"Who would that be?" Elizabeth asked, all innocence.

Bruce's face went red. "Come on, Liz. You know I'm first singles. All-county first singles, in case you haven't read any real newspapers lately. Why do you always cut me down?"

Because you need it so much! Elizabeth thought. But she said, "I was thinking of writing about

40

you. John Pfeifer is the sports editor, you know, but I was thinking of doing a feature story on the human side of tennis.''

"Really?"

The combination of *human* and Bruce Patman almost made Elizabeth gag, but the memory of Robin's unhappy face stiffened her resolve.

"Yes, I've been thinking of writing an article about somebody who would do a good deed for someone else and never tell another soul about it,'' she went on.

Bruce looked puzzled. He scratched his head. "I don't get you, Liz. What is it you want to write about? Me or a do-gooder?"

It was all going right by Bruce, Elizabeth realized. His selfish nature simply did not allow him to conceive of helping anyone except himself.

She was about to turn on her heel and stalk away. But Robin's face floated before her again. She'd have to spell it out for him.

"Bruce, listen. What if somebody did you a good deed? Would it make sense for you to do the other person a good deed in return?"

"Well—maybe. Depends on what it is."

"Just suppose that somebody wrote a story about you in *The Oracle*—"

Bruce smiled. "About being first singles—and

how I creamed that hotshot from Palisades High?"

"Yes—about that, too."

"And maybe about how John McEnroe is looking over his shoulder?"

It was definitely give-me-strength time. "Bruce, I—"

"What kind of a picture do you need?"

"Wait a minute, Bruce. If somebody wrote a story about you—"

"With a photo?"

"With a photo. Do you think you'd be willing to do that person a favor in return?"

"What favor?"

Elizabeth took a deep breath, held it for a moment, then let it out. "Take a certain girl to the Discomarathon next Saturday night?"

Bruce's reaction caught Elizabeth off guard. He smiled. He preened. He stood straight and gave her a sidelong glance.

"Sure. I'd be willing to take you, Liz."

"Me?"

"I always knew you were attracted to me. I've even noticed you, too."

Hold on, Elizabeth Wakefield cautioned herself sternly. *Don't say what you're thinking.*

"Bruce, that's nice of you," she said, smiling tightly. "But I already have a date." And then, barely able to force the words out, she added, "Would you take Robin Wilson to the dance?"

Bruce began to laugh.

"Bruce," Elizabeth interrupted him sternly, "I'm dead serious."

Bruce continued to chuckle for a moment as he studied Elizabeth's earnest expression. Then abruptly he stopped, replacing his smile with a furious glare.

"Fatso Wilson?"

Elizabeth cringed but went on. "It's a sorority obligation, Bruce. It will mean everything to Robin."

"No way! What will the guys think? What would the *girls* think? Who do you think I am?"

Elizabeth smiled. "You're first singles. By the way, who's second singles? Isn't it Tom McKay?"

"Second singles?"

"Hasn't he won all his matches this year, too?"

Bruce Patman spun his racket. He shook his head back and forth, struggling with a decision. Finally he spoke. "All right. I'll take her. But I want my picture in, see! A big one. And tell how I whipped that guy at Palisades."

"It's a deal." Elizabeth grinned. "You won't be sorry. You're doing something nice for a nice person."

"Save it, Liz. One of us is going to regret

this deal." Bruce turned toward his opponent. "Ready!"

The freshman lobbed a soft shot over the net toward Bruce's forehand. It was a mistake. Bruce's racket whizzed through the air and— *thonk*—the ball careened past the frozen freshman's astonished face.

By the time she got home, Elizabeth was feeling wonderful. Actually, she thought, it was kind of fun to pit her wits against Jessica and her sorority sisters—as long as she won, of course.

Jessica was bouncing down the steps in an ice-blue string bikini, heading for the backyard pool. With her slim body, she'd never suffer the miseries poor Robin had gone through that day at the beach. It wouldn't hurt Jessica to consider things like that once in a while. But that would be like asking frogs to fly.

"Well," Elizabeth said brightly, "how's Robin doing?"

Jessica feigned disinterest. "Oh, I don't know. She tries, but I'm not sure she's going to make it."

"Why not? She's done everything you've asked."

Jessica's smile was secretive and sly. "Yes—so far."

Elizabeth grinned. "If she's made it so far, I can't imagine anything stopping her now."

"Want to bet?"

"Bet what?"

"Two weeks of laundry?"

"You're on." Elizabeth grabbed Jessica's hand and pumped it to seal the bargain.

Jessica laughed.

Elizabeth laughed, too.

Then Jessica darted out through the back, and Elizabeth heard a splash as her sister dove into the pool. Jessica's triumphant laugh drifted back to Elizabeth as she started up the stairs. She stopped midway, however, when Lila Fowler walked into the house.

"Hi, Liz. Jessie here?"

"In the pool," Elizabeth said, then started upstairs again. But a nagging thought made her stop.

"Say, Lila, how's your aunt?"

"What aunt?"

"You know, the one from New York. The shopping freak?"

"Are you on weird pills, Liz? You're not making a whole lot of sense."

Patience, Elizabeth told herself.

"The generous New York aunt who showers

45

you with expensive gifts, Lila." *The gifts you pass along to my sister*, she added to herself.

Lila shrugged. "I don't know what you're talking about." Then, staring at Elizabeth, she suddenly seemed to change her mind. "Oh, that aunt. She's fine, thanks." Lila smiled unconvincingly.

As Lila nervously lifted her right hand to smooth her hair, Elizabeth spotted the ring.

"Wow, Lila—what a ring!"

"It's OK." Lila stretched out her hand to give Elizabeth a closer look.

Elizabeth examined the gold ring. It was magnificently crafted, with an Egyptian pharaoh's head carved on it.

Lila tapped her right foot impatiently. "I'd like to get out to the pool while the sun is still shining, Liz. Are you just about through looking at my ring?"

"Oh, yeah, sure, Lila."

As Lila went out to the pool, Elizabeth had an unsettling feeling. She was fairly certain there was no aunt in New York, so how had Jessica gotten the scarf and earrings? Was Lila just hiding her generosity—or trying to buy Jessica's friendship? There was probably a very simple explanation, Elizabeth attempted to assure herself. But deep down inside she had the distinct feeling there was trouble ahead.

Four

"Hello?"

"Robin, it's Liz Wakefield. Have you kept your promise?"

"What promise?"

"Have you asked Bruce Patman to the Disco-marathon?"

Silence.

"Robin?"

"Elizabeth, how can you make me do this? I'll be totally humiliated."

"Now you listen to me, Robin," Elizabeth said sternly. "I happen to know that Bruce *will* take you to the dance. He told somebody he would."

First there was a stunned silence. Then, "Who told you that? Who was it? How could anybody say that? How could Bruce say that? Who did Bruce tell that to? Oh, it can't be true! It's totally bananas!"

Elizabeth broke into laughter at Robin's outburst.

"How can you laugh at me?"

"Oh, Robin, I'm not laughing *at* you. I'm telling you, Bruce will take you. All you have to do is ask him."

"I'll swim to Hawaii first!"

The phone went dead.

Elizabeth didn't see Robin again until Monday at school, when she spotted her nervously ducking into the biology lab in an obvious attempt to avoid any questions. Elizabeth was about to follow Robin when she noticed Bruce. He was swaggering along toward the cafeteria, and Elizabeth quickly caught up with him.

"Did she ask you yet?"

"Naw. Is this whole thing a gag, Liz?"

"No. She'll ask you today."

"You got that story written?"

Elizabeth patted her tote bag. "It's right here."

*   *   *

It wasn't until after school on Tuesday that the Great Explosion happened. Liz was in the newspaper office typing her "Eyes and Ears" column when the door opened and in burst Robin Wilson.

"Elizabeth!"

Elizabeth looked up at Robin, and she got scared. Robin was clutching the back of a chair for balance, her face was as red as a boiled lobster, and she seemed to be gasping for breath.

"Robin, are you OK?"

"Elizabeth!"

And then Elizabeth knew. Smiling broadly, she jumped up from her typewriter.

"Omigod! He said yes!"

Elizabeth threw her hands up in the air, and Robin immediately began hugging her wildly. Elizabeth almost felt smothered as Robin, laughing and crying at the same time, danced her around the news office.

"He said yes! He said yes! He said yessss! Bruce Patman is taking me to the dance!"

And before Elizabeth could say another word, Robin was gone, flying out the door and down the hall on wings of bliss.

From Tuesday until Saturday, the phone rang constantly for Elizabeth. It was always Robin, pouring out her gratitude and happiness. "They'll all accept me now, Liz. A date with Bruce Patman! I love you for making me do it." It was clear Robin felt her world was finally in its proper orbit.

And Elizabeth began to worry again. Walking into the Discomarathon on the arm of Bruce Patman would not be Robin's passport to popularity. Elizabeth was sure of that. But Robin couldn't stop fantasizing about it. Hoping for the best, Elizabeth decided to tackle one problem at a time. Besides, right now she wanted the satisfaction of seeing Jessica's stunned expression.

"Guess who called?" Elizabeth smiled at her sister. "Robin. Our new pledge—who, by the way, is going to the dance with Bruce Patman tonight."

"Oh, Liz, will you please shut up about it!"

"So, you know that our Pi Beta pledge has landed such a coveted date?"

"Oh, my head is going to burst into at least five hundred and thirty-seven pieces!" Jessica raged. "How could such an incredible thing happen? It's like science fiction!"

"Maybe you can figure it out while you're doing the laundry for me. You won't forget the ironing, will you?"

Jessica stormed out of the room.

That Saturday night in the Sweet Valley High gym, Elizabeth thought everything seemed too perfect as she danced dreamily in Todd's arms. Feeling his strong, athletic body so close to her always made her feel warm, excited, and utterly in love. When he began to rub her back as they danced, Elizabeth could barely remember where she was.

Suddenly she heard a few people near the entrance giggling. When she looked up, she saw Robin coming in with Bruce Patman. Robin's face was absolutely radiant with happiness.

She swept in grandly, wearing a prettier tent dress than usual, passing the stony faces of the three conspirators. Jessica, Lila, and Cara had all stopped dancing and were glowering with rage and disbelief. Elizabeth found herself relieved that it was over at last. Now all she had to do was turn in the feature story about Bruce Patman's prowess on the tennis court to her editor at *The Oracle*, and the bargain would be complete. Finally, she'd have more time for herself and Todd.

Bruce led Robin onto the floor, and, as though in a movie, the other couples made way for them. A little circle opened in the center of the floor.

And then it happened. There was a momentary lull in the music, and Bruce's voice could be heard clearly as he stepped away from Robin, leaving her alone in the center of the floor.

"OK, that's it. I brought you to the dance, Tubby. I've got better things to do now. Hey! Anybody want to steer the *Queen Mary* around the floor tonight? She's all yours!"

And Bruce walked out.

Five

Robin stood there, alone, still, for what seemed like an eternity. Waves of humiliation washed over her. *Omigod*, she thought, *this can't be happening*. Not tonight. Not after everything she'd gone through in the past few weeks. She heard neither the embarrassed laughter nor the murmurs of pity from the surrounding crowd. Robin had only one thought in her mind now. And it was an overpowering one.

Snapping out of her shock, she frantically pushed through the crowd and headed for the entrance to the gym. Like an animal momentarily paralyzed by a bright light, once recovered, all she could think about was escape.

Elizabeth reached her just before she opened the door.

"Robin!"

"Leave me alone, Liz! I've got to get out of here!"

"Wait, Robin, come with me first." Firmly Elizabeth grabbed her hand and pulled the protesting Robin down a hall to the girls' room. Elizabeth didn't know who she was maddest at—Bruce Patman for being totally disgusting; Jessica, Lila, and Cara for thinking up the stunt; herself for bribing Bruce into going; or Robin for wanting to get into PBA so desperately in the first place.

Just as they reached the door of the girls' room, Enid Rollins, Elizabeth's best friend, caught up with them.

"Robin—Liz—is there anything I can do?" Good old Enid, Elizabeth thought. She could always be counted on.

"There sure is, Enid. Stand outside and guard this door. Don't let anyone in, especially not my sister and the other two witches."

Once inside, Robin broke down completely.

"Oh, Liz, I'm so ashamed!" she wailed. "I'll never be able to face anybody again. Never! My entire life is ruined!"

Elizabeth grabbed some paper towels from

the wall dispenser and ran cold water into one of the sinks.

"Here, put some water on your face. And stop talking like that. You didn't do anything to be ashamed of. If anybody should be ashamed, it's Bruce Patman—that rotten, egotistical creep!"

"Liz, it *is* my fault. How could I have been so totally stupid? Why would somebody who looks like Bruce Patman go out with somebody like me!" A fresh wave of tears ran down her cheeks.

"Just stop it right now, Robin Wilson!" Elizabeth snapped, hoping a tougher approach might work. "If you'd stop crying and feeling sorry for yourself for a minute, you might learn something."

"What could I possibly *learn*?"

"First of all, the only thing Bruce has going for him *really* is his looks. You happen to be lucky enough to have that and more."

"Liz, you must be out of your—"

"Look in the mirror," Elizabeth plowed on, determined to speak her mind. "Your eyes are kind of red and puffy now, but you've got a pretty face. A *very* pretty face."

"Look in the mirror?" Robin gasped, her shoulders still shaking with sobs.

"Yes, look," Elizabeth practically commanded, examining Robin more closely now. She had complimented Robin in order to cheer her up, but she saw now that it was true. Maybe it was the makeup and the care she'd taken with her hair. Whatever it was, Robin's face *was* lovely.

"Look in the mirror?" Robin repeated, fury edging into her voice. She turned to face Elizabeth. "I spend most of my life *not* looking in mirrors! I don't need a mirror to know what I look like. I'm fat and ugly. I may just be the fattest and ugliest girl in California!"

"Robin!"

"Don't 'Robin' me, Liz. You look in the mirror, and you see beauty. I look, and I see the beast."

"Robin, that's just not true."

"It is true, Liz. Sad but true." She grabbed her purse. "I'm getting out of here and going home right now!"

"Terrific, Robin. *That* will really impress Jessica."

"You think I could go back in there after what happened?" Robin demanded.

"Robin, I think you should do whatever you want to do. I'm just suggesting that running away isn't going to solve anything."

"And I'm telling you that staying certainly isn't going to solve anything!"

The door opened, and Enid stuck her head in.

"Hey, you two. I can't hold them off much longer. There's more dancing in the girls' room line than on the dance floor. I think they need to use something besides the mirror."

"We're coming, Enid. Thanks."

"I hear Todd's offered to rearrange Bruce Patman's face," Enid added, laughing.

"Omigod, look at the trouble I'm causing," Robin cried. "I can't go back to the dance! I can't even go back to school. I'm quitting! I should have done it before. I'll never come back to this school again!"

"Robin!"

Before Elizabeth could stop her, Robin squeezed by and ran out of the girls' room. Frantically she pushed her way down the crowded hall toward the front door.

"Liz, what's going on?"

"Not now, Enid. Not now."

Elizabeth had to dodge groups of people as she chased after Robin. Preoccupied with the problem of what she would say once she caught her friend, Elizabeth crashed into someone.

"Ouch!"

She looked up, and up. She had nearly knocked over the tallest, the smartest, and perhaps the shyest boy at Sweet Valley High. Allen Walters's one extracurricular activity was taking pictures for *The Oracle*. Other than that, he kept to himself.

"Allen, I'm sorry."

"No, Liz, it's probably my fault. I shouldn't have been in the way."

Inspiration struck Elizabeth. "Allen, you have to do something for me—right now. It's crucial!"

"Me? Now?"

"I don't have time to explain. I've got to stop Todd, and you have to stop Robin Wilson. She ran out the door. She's totally upset, and I'm worried about what she'll do!"

"Liz, I can't—"

"You have to, Allen! Trust me, it's important!" She gave him a shove in the direction of the front door, then hurried over to where Todd and Bruce were standing, glaring at each other, eyeball to eyeball. Discomarathon had become Discodisaster.

Robin was halfway across the parking lot before she realized someone was running after her.

"Robin! Hey, Robin, wait up!"

Frightened, Robin turned around. It was Allen Walters running toward her. Wasn't the evening bad enough without this?

"Why are you chasing me?" she demanded.

The harsh glare of the parking lot's neon lights revealed a belligerent Robin, standing with hands on hips. Allen stood before her, panting.

Surprised at his own brazen behavior, he muttered, "I guess I was chasing you, wasn't I?"

"Why?"

"Why?"

"You heard me, Allen. Why were you chasing me?"

"Gee, I don't know, Robin. I just—well, Liz Wakefield said that you were—and—I—" Allen looked down at his feet, unable to continue.

" 'I don't know—Liz Wakefield said—' " Robin mimicked. "Can't you put a sentence together, Allen? I thought you were supposed to be so smart."

"I thought you needed help, Robin," he blurted out.

"Help? Help!" Robin's rage was fast approaching a fever pitch. "Did you see what happened to me in there?"

"Well—uh—"

"I am a total outcast! I'm ruined!" Robin was nearly screaming.

"If I can—"

"If you can what? Help me? *You* are going to help me? *You* are going to somehow, magically, help me fit in? That's the biggest joke of the whole night!"

Allen's face turned red. "Hey, look, I'm sorry, Robin."

"Sorry? My whole world is falling down around me, and who offers to help me?" She looked up into the sky. "Allen Walters! Omigod!"

Allen edged away, head down. "I'd better go. I have some things to do at home. I—I'm sorry, Robin."

Robin watched him head off across the parking lot. The misery on Allen's face looked familiar to her. In her anger at the world, she had attacked an innocent bystander. She was no better than Bruce Patman.

"Allen, wait up! Please!"

Allen stopped and waited for Robin to catch up with him.

"Allen, I—look, I'm sorry. I shouldn't have yelled at you like that."

"It's OK. I shouldn't have butted in."

"What were you doing in there, anyway, Allen?"

"Hey, I go to school here, too, you know?"

Flustered, Robin blurted out, "It's just that— well, sure I know you go here, but I didn't think—I mean, I didn't know you went to *dances*."

Allen shrugged and looked up at the sky.

Robin was immediately contrite. "I didn't mean it like that, Allen. It's just that I'm used to seeing you in the library or the chem lab. I guess I didn't think you were interested in things like dances." *Wow!* she thought. *Can you stick your foot in any farther?*

"I guess I have to get out of the library once in a while," he said with bitterness. "I should have gone to the movies instead. I don't have a lot to say to people at dances."

"You, too?"

"I say a lot of dumb things at places like this," he admitted. "I like the movies—especially old movies. Did you know there's a Humphrey Bogart festival at the Valley Cinema? *There's* someone who always knew the right thing to say!"

Robin smiled for the first time in an hour. "Lauren Bacall always knew the right thing to say, too. Maybe we should get a scriptwriter."

Allen laughed. It was a nice laugh, Robin realized.

"Well, I guess I'd better get going, Robin."

"Going?"

"Yeah. I've got to get home."

"You're not going back to the dance?"

"Back there? No way. I didn't belong there in the first place."

Remembering Elizabeth's lecture, Robin took a deep breath. "You know, Allen, running away from a problem doesn't solve it."

"Huh?"

Robin paused, finding it hard to believe she

was trying to talk Allen Walters into going back to the one place she was determined to avoid. *I must be as out of it as everybody thinks I am*, she told herself.

"Maybe you should assert yourself, Allen. You have as much right to be there as anybody else."

Allen thought about that. "Maybe you're right. OK, let's go."

"Us?" Robin sputtered. "I meant you. I'm going home."

"I don't think I can go in there alone, Robin."

Running her fingers through her dark hair, Robin tried to imagine what would happen if she went back to the gym. *Oh, why not?* she finally concluded. The worst had to be over.

"One dance?" she said.

"I can if you can."

They both cringed a little as they reentered the gym. The noise, the lights, the crowd made a sharp, unfriendly contrast to the peace of the parking lot.

Just at that moment, Jessica swirled by. "Robin, PBA pledges are supposed to dance, to mingle—not to hide out in corners with . . ." The rest of her words were lost, but Robin got the message: PBA pledges do not hide out in corners with wimps like Allen Walters.

And then she was in Allen's arms, and they

were dancing. If it could be called that. He seemed to want to turn in only one direction, so they were constantly spinning backward. Robin glanced at him, and his face was red and grim. A little embarrassed for both of them, she looked over her shoulder again, only to see smirking faces watching them as they moved across the floor.

Robin wasn't the only one who noticed. At the end of the song, Allen muttered, "Listen, I have to get out of here. I'm just not much good at this."

"Sure," said Robin. "I understand. I'll see you around sometime." Wondering if Allen thought her dancing was as clumsy as his, she swiftly turned and headed for the door. She was going to do what she should have done all along—go home.

To her surprise Allen caught up with her again. "Say, can't I see you home?"

"What?"

"Well, I mean—"

"You want to?"

"Yeah, sure I do."

Robin smiled, surprised. "OK, Allen."

As they walked out, Robin glanced at Allen Walters again. He was even taller than she had realized. And he had very nice eyes.

Six

Jessica Wakefield was an innocent person wrongfully accused, she raged.

Elizabeth pursued her around her bedroom, knocking down Jessica's arguments at every turn.

"Elizabeth, I will not be yelled at for that ridiculous charade tonight! I mean, it's a total mystery how or why Bruce Patman took Robin to the Discomarathon at all. Nobody believed for a second that she'd ever get him to take her!"

"Oh, then you admit that you deliberately set up an impossible task so she couldn't make it into Pi Beta, huh?"

"Yes—no—that's not fair! If she were the right material for Pi Beta, she wouldn't have had any trouble. But, who ever thought—? Besides, *I* don't control Bruce Patman."

No, Elizabeth thought sourly, *I took care of that.*

Somehow Jessica sensed that she had struck a note that put her in the driver's seat. She immediately pressed forward.

"We all tried to figure out why Bruce did it, but we couldn't. Did you hear anything?"

"Me?"

"Yes. You seem to have taken over as Robin's best friend. Did she tell you how she worked that little miracle?"

"No," said Elizabeth. "Let's just drop it. I'm only glad Robin got through all this alive. At least you can't keep her out now."

Jessica sat before her mirror and began brushing her hair. "I'm tired," she said. "I'm going to bed."

"You heard me, didn't you? I said you can't keep Robin out now."

Jessica stared at her reflection as she brushed her sun-streaked, shoulder-length hair.

"You know, sister dear, I am not the entire membership of Pi Beta Alpha. It's not up to me alone."

Elizabeth didn't like the sound of that. But she was too exhausted to figure out what Jessica was really saying.

Elizabeth was so relieved that Robin's pledge dares seemed to be over that she didn't even mind when the next day Jessica ducked out, leaving her to pick up their mother's watch at the repair shop in the Valley Mall. It amused her to think how outraged Jessica would be when she discovered that Elizabeth had been allowed to drive her mother's little red Fiat for the errand.

She laughed to herself. *Too bad, Jessica. That's what you get for pulling your usual disappearing act.*

She parked the car, picked up the gold watch, and was strolling back through the vast, airy indoor mall when she spotted an exclusive little shop she hadn't noticed before.

The discreet sign over the door read Lisette's. The selection of imported, expensive French gifts in the window was breathtaking. Elizabeth found herself walking in to gaze at uniquely designed gold jewelry on display atop bright glass counters. Beautifully crafted gold earrings caught her eye, as did a gossamer-delicate pin, inlaid with precious stones. Lovely silk scarves, tied gracefully around a velvet post, cascaded onto the front counter.

Elizabeth undid one and examined it carefully. It was exactly like the one Lila Fowler had given to Jessica.

"Yes, miss?" said a polite voice. Elizabeth looked up to see a saleslady watching her warily.

"What a lovely scarf," Elizabeth commented.

"Yes," the saleslady said, moving closer. "May I interest you in one?"

"Oh, I was just looking. But—how much is it?"

She smiled. "It's one of our finest imports, and only ninety-five dollars."

Elizabeth felt the scarf slide from her hands. "Ninety-five dollars?" she repeated.

"They're an exclusive item with us, you see."

"Exclusive? You mean exclusive in California?"

"I mean exclusive anywhere."

"Oh, but a friend of mine . . ." Elizabeth began, her voice trailing off. So it was true. Lila's aunt couldn't have sent it to her. But Lila didn't seem like the type to purchase such generous gifts for her friends.

"Pardon me?"

"Nothing," Elizabeth mumbled.

"Have you seen a scarf like this somewhere else?"

"Oh, well—I thought I saw one like it."

In her nervousness Elizabeth moved away a little too suddenly, and a tray of gold jewelry went skittering across the glass counter.

"Oh, my goodness! Oh, I'm so sorry . . ."

She anxiously scooped up rings, earrings, and bracelets, hastily putting them back on the tray. As the saleslady began to rearrange the pieces into an attractive display, Elizabeth suddenly spotted another familiar item. It was a little face on a gold ring. A delicately carved Egyptian pharaoh's face. Exactly like the gold ring Lila Fowler had.

Lila certainly does believe in spending her money, Elizabeth thought.

The saleslady was now out from behind the counter, checking to see if any stray pieces of jewelry had fallen onto the floor.

"Please stay here, young lady, until I have everything," she said in a tone of voice that sounded more like a command than a polite request.

"What?"

"Let me see now. . . . Yes, that's right. I guess that's everything."

"What's the matter?"

"You might be interested to know that we have recently installed a brand-new, very expensive security system, young lady. Shoplifting isn't going to be so easy from now on."

"Shoplifting?"

"Yes. The shoplifter who has been working this mall—and my shop, in particular—had better watch out. In fact, that lovely scarf I saw you staring at has a twin. But it was one of the items that was taken."

"Yes ma'am," Elizabeth heard herself saying as her mind began whirling.

"Who is the person whom you said has a scarf like ours?"

"Oh," said Elizabeth, backing away. "I can't remember her name."

Moments later, she walked out of the mall, headed toward the Fiat Spider. *It's probably nothing*, she kept telling herself. *It must be a different scarf.* But the nagging feeling that someone was not telling a frightening truth kept returning.

Terrified of her own thoughts, she started the car.

Seven

The next morning Elizabeth was tired. She had been awake much of the night, unable to forget her suspicions. Should she confront Jessica about the gifts from Lila? Were they really *gifts*? If not, how had Jessica gotten them?

Go in there right now and ask her, she told herself. *Ask her what?* "Are you a shoplifter, Jess?" Elizabeth's worst fears were starting to take over. Jessica had done some pretty sneaky things, but she wouldn't steal—would she? Would Lila, when she had enough money to buy anything her heart desired?

Try the casual approach. "Hey, Jess, pick anything

up at the Valley Mall lately that you forgot to pay for?" "What a dumb idea," Elizabeth muttered to herself. *Maybe I should tell Mom? After all, aren't parents supposed to handle things like this? Sure. Great. "Mom, I think Jessica may be shoplifting at the mall. Have a nice day!"* That wasn't a dumb idea. That was a totally idiotic idea.

"Lizzie, what do you think?" Jessica burst into Elizabeth's room without bothering to knock. Jessica never considered privacy important—except her own.

"I think I don't know whether I want to be my brother's keeper," Elizabeth answered.

"You know what I think? I think you're strange. Steve doesn't need a keeper."

"Steve?"

"You remember him: tall, two years older than we are, comes home from college once in a while. Why in the world would he need your help?" Jessica drawled sarcastically.

Elizabeth stared at her sister in momentary confusion. "Steve? Oh, for heaven's sake, Jess. When I said brother, I didn't mean *our* brother. I was speaking about—I was just speaking philosophically," she finished hurriedly.

"Don't get weird on me, Liz. I only came in to ask you if my new scarf goes with this sweater. I don't need a philosophy lecture."

Elizabeth stared at Jessica's sapphire scarf and

heaved a tense sigh. "About that scarf—" she began, then faltered. "Actually, Jess"—a germ of an idea suddenly formed—"the scarf isn't really right for you. It makes your skin look sort of yellowish!"

"Yellowish?" Jessica squeaked and spun around to look in the mirror. She ripped the offending scarf off and dropped it on Elizabeth's dresser. "You might have had the decency to tell me about this before, instead of letting me walk around with a yellow face!"

Thoroughly annoyed, Jessica was almost out the door when her sister's question abruptly stopped her.

"By the way, Jess, what time is the PBA meeting tonight?"

"Meeting—tonight?"

"Jessica, I know tonight is vote night."

"Vote?"

Give me strength, Elizabeth pleaded to whatever forces might be listening.

"I know that Robin and the two other pledges will be voted on tonight, Jess. Where and what time?"

"I don't know how you found out about it. Eight o'clock—Cara Walker's house!"

"What do you mean you don't know how? It's my right to vote! You couldn't call it a final count without me!"

"Oh, I was going to do you the favor of voting for you," Jessica answered sweetly. "I know how you dislike going to the meetings."

Elizabeth shook her head in disgust at her sister. Well, at least the Robin Wilson problem would be resolved, she thought. "When will you induct Robin into PBA?"

"Induct? Haven't you forgotten something, Liz? The vote comes first."

"Jessica, she got through the pledging with flying colors. The vote should be automatic," Elizabeth reminded her.

"Maybe," Jessica returned. "Gee, look at the time. We'll be late if we don't get a move on." She practically flew down the stairs.

"Jessica!" Elizabeth shouted. "You'd better not be planning anything."

"Who me?" an indignant voice floated up to the second floor.

Elizabeth folded the scarf neatly and put it in her drawer before going downstairs. It seemed a good idea to hide it, though she wasn't sure what good it would do her in the end.

"Elizabeth, what is the significance of the Dred Scott case?" asked Mr. Fellows, her history teacher.

"What do I dread? What—what did you say?"

Elizabeth stammered, to the merriment of the class.

"When you return to earth, let me know," said Mr. Fellows. He then directed the same question to Todd Wilkins.

After class, a concerned Todd caught up with Elizabeth. "You really look spaced out," he said.

"Oh, Todd! Things are in such a mess."

"What happened?"

"Well—I just know it's not true."

"What's not true?"

"But I know it *is*."

"Huh?"

"I'll see you later," she said and hurried off, leaving Todd standing alone, shaking his head.

That day Elizabeth made a firm decision to tell everything to Mr. Collins. Then she decided just as firmly not to. She would simply forget about it all. Then she realized that was impossible. She had to find out the truth.

The battle in her head concerning Jessica's involvement with the stolen goods gave Elizabeth such a headache that it was a relief to go to the sorority meeting that night at Cara Walker's house on the hill. *At least this problem will finally be resolved*, she assured herself as she walked in a few minutes later.

The little red lacquered wooden box was already being passed around the room, and Elizabeth hurriedly grabbed a handful of marbles and took her seat. It was so quiet the girls could all hear the sharp clack of the marbles as they were dropped into the hole in the lid, one by one.

"Suzanne Hanlon," Jessica said for Elizabeth's benefit as she watched Cara hand the lacquered box to Lila Fowler.

Lila dropped her marble in, and the little box moved on, from one pair of hands to the next, until it completed a circle and was once again in Jessica's hands.

Jessica opened the box and poured out the marbles. They were all white.

"Suzanne Hanlon is in," said Jessica, and everyone applauded.

"She's totally acceptable," Lila whispered to Elizabeth. "And you know her father has a Rolls-Royce."

Jessica had already closed the lid of the red box and was about to send it on another round.

"Robin Wilson," she said, and Elizabeth detected a sarcastic note. Jessica avoided Elizabeth's eyes, dropped her marble in, and sent the box along.

Elizabeth carefully separated the white and the black marbles in her hands, then dropped a white one in when the box came to her. She handed it on to the next girl and breathed a sigh of relief when the box had completed its rounds.

Jessica opened the box. "Uh-oh," she said.

"What's the matter?" Lila asked, with Cara echoing her question.

Jessica reached into the box and brought out a marble between her thumb and forefinger. She held it up. "Blackball!" she said.

Astonished looks flashed across the faces of the Pi Betas as they looked around at each other.

"Robin Wilson has been blackballed!" Jessica announced. "She can't be a member of PBA."

A hushed and embarrassed silence followed her pronouncement. Jessica and her sister had wanted Robin Wilson in, and now somebody had blackballed her. Sure, Robin was a loser. But who would dare to cross Jessica this way?

"Who could it be?" the girls whispered among themselves, silently considering each other's possible motives.

A stunned Elizabeth sat perfectly still, consumed with anger. There was only one person who would have the nerve to keep Robin out. Jessica!

The other girls were now crowding around Jessica, voicing their sympathy over her friend Robin's exclusion from the sorority. And Jessica, it seemed to Elizabeth, was taking it very well. Wonderfully well.

"Who could have done such a thing?" Elizabeth hissed sarcastically at Jessica when no one else was listening.

Jessica smiled. "I can't imagine. But it's a secret vote—and nobody can challenge a blackball. It's just one of those unfortunate things."

Already the whisper was circulating. How would Robin take the bad news? By now everyone knew that her whole existence depended on making PBA. There could be a really awful scene if she found out at the next general meeting, when membership announcements were usually made.

The expression on Jessica's lovely face was that of a martyr facing the lions in the Roman Colosseum. "I'll tell her personally," she said oh-so-bravely. "She's my friend. It's my responsibility."

"I'll go with you," volunteered Elizabeth quickly. "Somebody had better be there to pick up the pieces."

Robin hurried eagerly into Casey's Place in the Valley Mall that evening to keep the date with Jessica. "I'll come right away," she had gushed when Jessica called.

Robin headed for their booth as soon as she came in. "I ran right out the door," she bubbled, her face flushed with excitement. "I just couldn't wait to get here."

It was only when Robin sat down that she noticed that Jessica was not smiling, although she certainly wasn't grim. She was composed.

"Robin, I want you to know first of all that we will always be friends," Jessica said.

Robin's face began to change. "What—?"

"We will still be the best of friends. If I need somebody to keep me company while I run errands, I'll still ask you first."

"Jessica, what are you saying?"

"Robin, you were blackballed," said Jessica, in a tone that reminded Elizabeth of the purr of a satisfied cat.

Robin was as white as chalk. As Jessica's message sank in, her eyes widened into a stare filled with pain, and long-suppressed anger.

"But they can't!" she screamed, tears of frustration falling from her eyes.

"I know you feel it leaves you out of everything worth having at Sweet Valley High," said Jessica sweetly, "but I'll still be your best friend."

Elizabeth couldn't believe her ears. "Oh, Jess, shut up!"

"What? Shut up?" Jessica cried plaintively.

"It can't be happening," Robin cried. "I did what you asked. I don't deserve this!"

"Some things were just not meant to be,"

Jessica said with such mock sweetness that Elizabeth thought she was going to be sick.

Elizabeth reached over the table, trying to find some words of comfort for Robin, but Robin pulled away, threw herself against the back of the booth, and glared at them wild-eyed.

"Don't touch me! I can't stand it!" She slid out of the booth, stood up, lurched against a chair, and looked back at the twins. Her face was contorted with suffering and fury.

"There isn't any reason for me to go on," she said hoarsely, and then she rushed out, knocking over a chair.

"Are you satisfied?" Elizabeth snapped at her sister.

"Oh, for heaven's sake, Liz," Jessica replied sourly. "She didn't mean what it sounded like."

Elizabeth got up. "I'm not so sure, Jessica. People can just take so much. . . ."

Eight

For the rest of the evening Elizabeth tried continually—and unsuccessfully—to get in touch with Robin.

"What happened?" Robin's mother pleaded when Elizabeth called her.

"The Pi Betas blackballed her, Mrs. Wilson."

"Oh, no! She was counting on it so much."

"I know. I'm the one who sponsored her."

"How can young people be so cruel?" Mrs. Wilson said softly.

"I really don't know, Mrs. Wilson," Elizabeth answered truthfully. Why Jessica, Lila, and Cara would work so hard to keep Robin out of their sorority bewildered her. And that Robin would let herself be humiliated to join such a bunch of snobs seemed just as mysterious.

Elizabeth was sitting in the *Oracle* office the next day, her fingers resting quietly on the typewriter keys. She was trying to think of what to write, but one question kept intruding: *Why is it some people can enjoy being so mean?*

"Five dollars for your thoughts." It was Roger Collins, the newspaper adviser, who had noticed her staring at the blank paper in her typewriter.

No response.

"OK, so forget the attempt at inflation humor," he said. "What's on your mind, Liz?"

"Mr. Collins, why would people who have just about everything—good looks, popularity, money—why would people like that want to hurt somebody else by excluding them?"

"Excluding them?" asked Mr. Collins. "How?"

"From an 'in' group. A sorority."

"Well, Elizabeth, what do you think?"

"I just can't understand it. As a matter of fact, as far as I'm concerned, *those* people are the deprived ones. Where's their kindness, their compassion? It's almost as if they're afraid they'll fall apart if they help anyone."

"What do you mean, Elizabeth?"

"Well, maybe that's the only way they can feel superior. Mr. Collins, sometimes I think the only way they keep themselves special is by keeping other people out."

"Hmm. Sounds like an article for *The Oracle*." Mr. Collins smiled encouragingly at Elizabeth and walked out of the office. Again, resting her fingers on the keys, a tentative Elizabeth finally began to work.

She found herself writing a spirited article entitled, "Snobbery Is Alive and Well at Sweet Valley High." It took her only an hour to complete, and she immediately gave it to Penny Ayala, the editor.

Elizabeth knew it was a public apology to Robin Wilson and a slap at the Three Witches of Pi Beta Alpha.

The day the article appeared, Elizabeth proudly read it several times. She thoroughly enjoyed the sour faces on some of the Pi Betas.

Her only disappointment was that Robin wasn't in school to see it; nobody had seen or talked to Robin since the blackball. Although Elizabeth had tried to reach her on the phone, Robin's mother kept insisting she was away and would probably be in touch when she got back. Elizabeth didn't like the sound of it.

Nor did she like the thought of discussing the awful mess with Jessica. She knew she'd get nowhere. But her "Snobbery at Sweet Valley" article brought things to a head. The day it came out, Jessica stormed into Elizabeth's room, waving *The Oracle*, fire flashing from her eyes.

"How could you?" she demanded. "Everybody in the entire state of California knows you're talking about me!"

"Well, at least I got that part clear." Elizabeth smiled in a way she knew would infuriate her sister.

"But we're *not* snobs!" Jessica screamed. "It's not our fault that everybody wants to join us. We can't take in everybody—we can't take in unsuitable people."

"So why did you encourage Robin and then knife her in the back, Jessica? Would you kindly tell me that?"

"*I* encouraged her? If I told her once, I told her eight hundred and thirty-seven times that blimps were not popular people!"

"Yes, you insulted her all the time. But you made her believe you would take her in sooner or later."

"That's not fair, Elizabeth Wakefield Buttinski!

Who sponsored that fatso? Who put her name up?"

Elizabeth felt her face getting red and her arguments becoming scrambled. As always, Jessica could tell when she was feeling defensive. She stepped up her attack.

"You put her up! You—Miss Goody-Goody!"

"Yes, but you let her believe she was your best friend," Elizabeth countered.

"Accepting her offer to carry my cleaning was hardly encouraging her."

"I'm sorry, Jessica, but it was just horrible of you to tell her she had to get a date with Bruce Patman!"

"Is that so?" Jessica said circling her sister like a lion moving in on its prey. "Is that so? That's what really got her hopes up, isn't it? Bruce taking her to the dance?"

"Yes—I guess so."

"You guess so? And who put the fix in with Bruce Patman? Huh, double-dealer?"

"What do you mean?"

"What do I mean?" Sarcasm was positively dripping from Jessica's tongue. "Elizabeth Wakefield, don't pretend with me. I happen to know that *you* conned Bruce Patman into taking Robin to the dance. *You* did all this—not us!"

"Who told you that?" Elizabeth managed to say weakly.

"I got it almost straight from the horse's mouth. A thoroughbred named Bruce Patman told Cara."

What a fool I was to trust a rat like Bruce, Elizabeth thought. Well, at least there was the small satisfaction of knowing her ego-stroking article about him had never seen the light of day. She'd torn it to shreds before it ever went to print.

"He's not going to let himself look like a total fool, even though we both know he's the biggest one Sweet Valley High has ever seen. Everybody knows he took Robin to the dance because you talked him into it. My own sister."

"Listen, Jessica, maybe I shouldn't have meddled. But I'm worried about Robin. Nobody's seen her for days. What's happening to her?"

"I don't know, and I don't care. She's not our problem anymore. We're all snobs. Remember? And if that lardo does anything to make me look bad, I'll never do another favor for her— ever!" And Jessica stormed out of the room.

Finally, the next day Elizabeth got a phone call from Mrs. Wilson, to let her know about Robin. She'd gone to Los Angeles to visit an aunt, but she was back.

"How is she, Mrs. Wilson?"

"I can't really say, Elizabeth. I'm only calling because I knew you were worried, and it seems my daughter doesn't want to speak with anyone."

"Can I at least try?"

"I especially don't think she wants to have anything to do with you or anyone else in your sorority. I don't mean to hurt you, dear, but I must respect Robin's feelings." And she hung up.

Elizabeth spotted Robin after school the next day and immediately noticed a change. Gone was the open, friendly face and the eager, quick step. Robin wore no makeup now and was dressed in a drab blue tent dress that seemed a little too big for her. As she walked, Robin looked only straight ahead, as though the rest of the world didn't exist for her. She moved through the corridors of Sweet Valley High as though she were a stranger there. The enthusiastic old Robin Wilson seemed to have vanished.

"Robin, I want to talk to you," Elizabeth pleaded, catching up with her in the front of the school. Robin turned to face her with a look that seemed to cut right through her.

Elizabeth shivered.

"Yes?" Robin said in a sharp, challenging tone. She stopped and stood perfectly still, staring with unwavering eyes at Elizabeth, who began to feel like a bug pinned to the wall.

"Robin, I just wanted you to know how sorry I am."

"Is that all?"

"Robin, don't be like this. Don't let those— don't let them get to you."

"It's too late, Elizabeth. I'm sorry to say they did get to me. But don't worry. I'm fine now."

Suddenly Jessica came through the doors and seeing them, hurried over. Her face was wreathed with sympathy.

"Robin," she gushed. "Oh, I'm so happy to see you! I want to tell you . . ."

Jessica's words evaporated on her lips. Robin had walked away.

"Well, did you see that?" Jessica fumed. "Of all the ungrateful, impossible—! Elizabeth Wakefield, what are you smiling at!"

During the following hectic few weeks, Elizabeth saw Robin from time to time walking through the halls of the school. Always she focused straight ahead, not speaking to anyone, as though she were willing herself to be alone, to disappear. She even began to look different, though Elizabeth couldn't figure out what was changing. She was clearly a new person, and

Elizabeth just didn't know whether it was for better or worse.

Something also happened with Lila Fowler. Elizabeth had noticed that Lila was dressing more and more wildly, wearing elaborate jewelry and extremely flashy clothes. At the same time, she seemed less involved with her friends and more interested in sounding off on her own desires and, as Elizabeth suspected, fantasies.

"I might be transferring," she said mysteriously one day. "I might go to school in the East."

"Where?" Jessica asked, wide-eyed.

"New York," said Lila. "My father knows the head of the American Academy of Dramatic Arts. I just may go there."

"Really?" Jessica was impressed.

"Actually, my father wants me to go to the Sorbonne in Paris," Lila went on. "He spends most of his time planning my future. It's really wonderful to have a father who wants to spend every minute with you."

Jessica filled Elizabeth's ears with Lila's extraordinary plans at every opportunity. Lila Fowler was not only the richest and one of the most beautiful girls at Sweet Valley High, it seemed to Jessica, but she also had the most adoring, generous father.

"Is she still giving you things?" Elizabeth asked.

"Yes, sometimes," Jessica said. "Are you jealous, Liz?"

"No," Elizabeth replied flatly. "Worried" would have been the better word, though she didn't say so.

"Do you like them?" Jessica asked, flicking the earrings that dangled attractively against her blond hair. Elizabeth took one between her fingers and looked at it. It was an exquisite, carefully detailed gold butterfly hanging from a delicate gold chain. Clearly very expensive. It was time for a showdown with her twin sister.

"Jessica, where did you get those earrings?" Elizabeth demanded.

"I told you—from Lila. Her aunt—"

"I asked Lila about her aunt in New York— and she's not a very good liar. I don't believe there's any such aunt, Jessica, so let's drop that."

Jessica turned an expression of total defiance toward her. "What are you saying, Liz?"

"Is that your story? Lila gave them to you?"

"It's the only story I know," Jessica snapped.

"You didn't get them yourself? From some-where. Maybe at the mall?"

"I couldn't afford these earrings, and you know it. They probably cost fifty or sixty dollars."

"Jessica, they probably cost two hundred and

fifty dollars! Will you wake up? Something's crazy here."

"Elizabeth, I will not listen to any more. Lila said her aunt gave them to her, and she gave them to me. What am I supposed to do—throw them back in her face? Anyway," Jessica rushed on, "maybe Lila just likes to buy me presents and was too embarrassed to admit it. She doesn't like to flaunt her money," Jessica added, knowing full well that wasn't true. She simply wanted to keep the gifts and was desperately searching for a good reason to do so.

"Jessica, I want your word—your absolute, solemn word—that you didn't . . . take them from someplace."

Jessica looked completely stunned. But a moment later, her shock turned to intense indignation as she considered what her twin had suggested.

"Elizabeth, that's too much! I'm going to tell Mom!"

"No, no, Jessie. Don't. It's OK—I believe you. I'm only worried, that's all. I didn't mean it."

Elizabeth quietly berated herself for being so suspicious of everyone. Maybe she was just tired these days, with so many things on her mind. Todd had complained at the Dairi Burger the day before that she always seemed off in another world. He had sounded annoyed, which was unusual for him. It seemed that she was upsetting everyone these days.

The day after her confrontation with Jessica, Elizabeth decided to make it up to Todd by getting him a special gift for his birthday. She had noticed that at basketball practice he tossed his wristwatch onto his sweat shirt lying on the sidelines because the watchband had worn through. She'd get him a really nice new band.

Hurrying through the mall after school, she headed for a little jeweler's shop where she had seen a selection of rich, dark leather watchbands in the window. They had the warm, masculine quality she associated with Todd. As she was about to enter the store, something caught her eye. An oddly dressed young woman was standing in Lisette's studying the counters. She was wearing a pair of bright green, skin-tight pants and a loose striped blouse that looked as though it could accommodate two people.

The young woman's back was facing her, but Elizabeth saw her palm a gold bracelet while the saleslady wasn't looking. She slipped the bracelet into her pocket, then turned and strolled away. For the first time Elizabeth had a clear view of her.

The thief had been brazen, stealing almost openly, as though she didn't care whether or not she were caught. As she strolled away, there was an absolutely calm expression on Lila Fowler's face.

Nine

Elizabeth forgot all about buying Todd's watch-band. As if hypnotized, she followed her sister's friend in silence.

Lila Fowler strolled casually through the mall without looking back and kept her hand in the pocket that held the stolen bracelet. Elizabeth numbly trailed her as far as the entrance arch and then watched her get into her lime green Triumph. Only when Lila's car was completely out of sight did Elizabeth come out of her trance-like state.

"This is too much for me," she blurted out loud as she retraced her steps back to the jeweler's shop.

As she got closer, she saw the saleslady at Lisette's frantically checking the jewelry on her counter. Clearly upset, the woman looked around anxiously, and her gaze fell upon Elizabeth, who seemed to be lingering outside.

"Hey—hey, there—you!"

It was like a scene from a tragic movie, Elizabeth thought later, where an innocent person unwittingly becomes implicated in a crime. Overwhelmed with fright, Elizabeth hurried around a corner of the mall and then, taking deep breaths, forced herself to walk home at a normal pace.

But being safely at home could not erase the terrible secret she had just uncovered. Lila Fowler was the shoplifter! Lila, probably the richest girl at Sweet Valley High! Here was a girl whose father gave her everything she ever wanted! A girl envied by all. Why did she do it?

Resting in her room, Elizabeth tried to sort out the reasons Lila would resort to stealing. She also tried to rid herself of the anger she felt for having to know about Lila in the first place. Elizabeth willed it to go away. Unfortunately, it couldn't be ignored. Not for long.

And she didn't know what to do.

Elizabeth suddenly became aware that she'd been able to question Jessica about the stolen items because she hadn't really thought Jessica had taken anything. But confronting Lila was a whole different thing, and Elizabeth trembled at the idea of handling the problem on her own.

She had no idea what Lila might do if confronted. The possibilities were alarming—and endless. She finally decided to do nothing, hoping the problem would go away.

A wave of guilt raced through her now as she remembered how she had suspected Jessica. She got up from her bed, walked into Jessica's room, and hugged her. There were tears in her eyes.

"I'm sorry, Jessie," she murmured. "You're a great sister."

Jessica looked at her twin in confusion. "What's the matter? What happened?" she asked, instinctively sensing a crisis.

"Nothing, Jess. I'm just sorry I suspected you of doing something you didn't do."

"Well, I'm glad you realize that, anyway. Robin Wilson was *your* doing!"

"OK," Elizabeth said, too tired to quarrel. Speaking of Robin, she hadn't seen much of her lately. "How is Robin, Jessie?"

"I don't know why you would ask me! Elizabeth, that girl has turned weird!"

"What do you mean?"

"Have you noticed her walking through the hall? She dresses like—I don't know what—like a gypsy. She's pale as a ghost, and I swear she acts like she's on something."

"Robin? Come on, Jess."

"Liz," said Jessica, her voice dropping dramatically to a whisper, "Liz, she looks right through me!"

Elizabeth had to agree. She had noticed that odd, vacant expression, too.

"And you know what else?" Jessica went on. "You know how we made her run the track? Well, she still does it—all the time."

That was true. Elizabeth had seen a solitary figure out on the track morning after morning, in baggy gray sweat clothes. Running, running, running.

"Yes, I've seen her."

"Liz, what's she doing? I hope this—this thing you made her do hasn't twisted her mind or something." Jessica seemed quite perturbed.

"I'll talk to her," Elizabeth said, then sighed.

"Would you, Liz? You know how to do things like that. And I just can't. I'm sure she's going off the deep end."

Elizabeth accepted Jessica's attitude that Robin Wilson was now her responsibility. She didn't forget that Robin had been Jessica's "best friend" and that it was the Pi Beta hazing and cruelty that had apparently affected Robin so deeply. But as it often happened with the Wakefield twins, Jessica worked very hard to convince herself and others that nothing that went wrong was her fault, while Elizabeth usually found herself having to mop up the mess, no matter who had caused it.

"But, Jessica, there's one thing I want you to do."

"Sure, Lizzie. Anything."

"Stay away from Lila Fowler!"

"What?"

"And don't accept any gifts from her—no matter what they are or where she says they came from."

"What? Why?"

"Trust me."

"Elizabeth, you can't just ask me to discard my very best friend and not tell me why. Are you still jealous of Lila? Why are you so hateful and mean to her?"

"Jessica, do you believe I love you? I'm your sister, and I want things to be good for you. I think Lila is heading for big trouble, and I'm afraid of the effects it'll have on you."

Elizabeth realized, too late, that she had opened up a Pandora's box. Jessica immediately became extremely agitated, practically shouting questions at her sister, not even pausing for the answers. "What do you mean? What have you heard? How could you be so vile? Since when do you know Lila so well?"

"I can't answer you," Elizabeth replied firmly but reluctantly. She refused to say more. She was sure of her conviction that telling Jessica everything would be a very dangerous move. Jessica insisted angrily that her sister leave her room, and a very sorrowful Elizabeth obliged her. Jessica's fury was a burden she would just have to bear alone.

Early the next morning Elizabeth walked to the track behind Sweet Valley High, and there was the solitary figure running in sweat clothes.

Elizabeth sat in the bleachers and waited.

Robin was like a machine on the track. She looked strong, almost athletic. And, as always these days, she stared straight ahead, blotting out everything else. She ran relentlessly, and it occurred to Elizabeth that perhaps she was running toward something, something only she could see.

Finally, Robin trotted over to the bleachers and stopped. She looked at Elizabeth calmly.

"You must have run a mile," Elizabeth said hesitantly.

"Five miles."

"Robin, I know it's none of my business, but how are you doing?"

"Fine. In fact, super. Do you remember when we had to read *The Iliad*? Remember the part where the Greeks and Trojans came under the spell of one of the gods?"

"Excuse me?" Elizabeth stammered, wondering if Robin really was falling apart.

"You should read it over again," Robin said. "Especially the part where the person comes out of the spell and finally sees clearly."

"You're not angry at me anymore?"

"Angry? I should thank you. You're the only one of that bunch I would even talk to. But honestly, Liz, I really can't talk right now. See you later."

And off she jogged toward the gym.

The conversation left Elizabeth more perplexed than ever, though one thing was for sure. Robin didn't seem depressed. She was different, all right, but not in a negative way. Elizabeth was intrigued. Her reporter's mind began searching for some clue that would explain what was taking place.

One day she walked through the cafeteria

and sat down at a table to wait for her friend Enid. Looking around, she saw Robin sitting alone at a nearby table. Elizabeth started to speak but quickly changed her mind. The clue she had been searching for was right in front of her.

Robin's plate, usually heaped with french fries and double burgers, now held only lettuce leaves, two tomato slices, and a hard-boiled egg. Elizabeth watched her silently, and when Robin got up to walk away, she noticed it for certain. On the track in bulky sweat clothes it wasn't obvious. But now, even in a tent dress, it was: Robin Wilson was losing weight.

Every day before classes Elizabeth checked behind the school and always saw the lone figure circling the track in her sweat suit. Every lunchtime she noticed a subdued Robin looking a little tired and very alone, picking at a scaled-down lunch. One day a week or two later Elizabeth almost bumped into her coming down the stairs—and was astonished to realize the transformation that was occurring. The excess pounds were going rapidly, and the Robin who was emerging seemed like an entirely different girl. Elizabeth remembered the night of the dance—Discodisaster—when she first realized that Robin had a pretty face. Now, as the weight fell away, that face was becoming more than just pretty.

Elizabeth grinned excitedly. "Robin, you're really losing weight."

"Very observant," Robin responded, a note of sarcasm in her voice.

"I hope you're doing it the right way Robin."

Robin fixed her penetrating eyes on Elizabeth, "Liz, I may have been stupid about almost everything—the Pi Betas, Jessica, and maybe even you. But if you're asking me if I'm starving myself to death, I wouldn't give any of the PBAs the satisfaction."

"Oh, Robin, I think you're terrific."

The expressionless eyes seemed to glow with a momentary warmth, but then the mask returned. Nodding a goodbye, Robin hurried down the stairs.

All the way home, Elizabeth found herself humming, her thoughts now on Todd. She'd been neglecting him shamefully lately, but she'd make it up to him.

The phone was ringing as she entered the house, and she ran to pick it up before it stopped. A breathless Lila Fowler was on the other end.

"Liz! Something terrible has happened."

"Lila, what's the matter? Where are you?"

"Liz, I'm at the mall. It's awful!"

"What, Lila? What happened?"

"It's Jessica. She's been arrested for shop-lifting!"

Ten

Driving to the mall, Elizabeth tried to stay calm. Painful questions were whirling around in her mind. Was Jessica shoplifting after all? Were she and Lila in on it together? Were they covering for each other?

She zipped into the mall parking lot and stopped near Lila Fowler's car. Lila had been standing beside it, pacing back and forth anxiously. Immediately she came running over to Elizabeth, her face grim. She dabbed at her eyes with a tissue.

"Liz, what are we going to do?"

Elizabeth got out of the car. "Where's Jessica?"

"They've got her—in there." Lila pointed un-helpfully in the general direction of the mall.

"Who's got her?"

"The detectives—the security people!"

"Lila, please calm down. Tell me what hap-pened."

"You've got to get her out of there, Liz. I—I can't stay."

"What?"

"You handle it, Liz. I've got to get home." Lila put her hand to her forehead and looked away from Elizabeth.

"You're not going anywhere, Lila Fowler," snapped Elizabeth. "Let's get that straight right now!"

Lila broke down completely then, slumping against the car and hiding her face. "I didn't know Jessie was taking things—I swear I didn't!"

"What did she take?"

"I don't know," Lila said, straightening up. "We just walked in today, and the next thing I knew two men walked up and grabbed her."

"You mean she hadn't taken anything? They just arrested her?"

"Yes! They said they've been waiting for her to come back—that she'd stolen things earlier."

Elizabeth felt a fury rising inside of her as she suddenly understood what had happened. The salesclerk at Lisette's had been watching for her, not Jessica.

"Oh, no! They wanted me!"

"You, Elizabeth? *You've* been taking things, too?"

Elizabeth fought the urge to grab Lila and shake her mercilessly. *What a total, absolute mess!* she screamed to herself. *Why didn't I remember to warn Jessica to stay away from the mall? Jessica wouldn't steal. I'm sure of that.*

"Lila, stop it, and listen to me! I know the truth."

Lila Fowler looked away and started twisting the tissue. "What do you mean?"

"I saw you steal a bracelet one day."

"A—bracelet?"

"Oh Lila, stop it! You've been lifting things from the mall!"

"What are you talking about, Elizabeth Wakefield?"

"Come off it, Lila."

Lila tried desperately for an air of outraged dignity. "My father is the richest man in Sweet Valley. He can buy me anything. I may even go study in Paris. I—"

"Lila, forget it. I said I *saw* you!"

"You . . . did?"

"Yes. You walked out with a gold bracelet.

And you've been giving Jessie things: a scarf, earrings, and I don't know what else."

Lila began to cry. The richest girl in Sweet Valley completely lost her composure and hid her face in her hands. "Oh, Liz, I'm so ashamed."

"But why, Lila? Why would you do such a crazy thing?"

"I don't know."

"Your father *can* buy you these things, can't he?"

"Yes, but that's all."

"What do you mean, 'that's all'?"

Lila wiped at the tears on her face. She looked over to the parking lot, and when she began to talk, it was with a bitterness Elizabeth had never heard before.

"You and Jessica are lucky. Your father spends time with you. And your mother, too. My mother took off right after the divorce, and I never see my father, even though we're supposed to be living in the same house. He's always too busy. Flying off to New York, to Paris, to Japan, or working late."

"He's a very important man, Lila."

"Sure! Big deal! When I was in *Pippin* at school last year, where was he? I'm a cheerleader, but he's never seen me at a game."

"Is that why you were stealing, Lila? To get his attention?"

106

"I don't know—maybe. But now I realize I can't ever let him know what I've done. You've got to get me out of this, Liz."

Elizabeth shook her head, wondering why she was always the one people turned to when things got tough. "Why me, Lila? I can't wave a magic wand and make everything all better!"

"Because you're the only one I can trust, Liz. You won't spread it all over. You're the only true friend I have."

Elizabeth wanted to remind her about Jessica, but what was the point?

"Come on. We've got to go in there and tell them the truth, Lila."

Lila shrank back in terror. "No! They'll tell my father!"

"You want Jessie to take the blame?"

"You'll get her out of it, Liz."

"On your feet! Let's go!"

Reluctantly, Lila walked toward the mall, pleading and crying every step of the way.

"Listen," Lila said, dragging Elizabeth into a corner just inside the mall. "I'll tell the truth, but can we at least fix it so my father doesn't have to know? I'll pay them, Liz. You can tell them I'll make it worth their while. Just keep my father out of it."

"Sorry, Lila." Elizabeth stood firm, though she felt pity for the desperate girl. "You've got to tell your father. But before we do anything else, we've got to get Jessica out of there."

"Elizabeth, promise me one thing? Please? Oh, you have to!"

"What is it?"

"Promise?"

"If I can."

"Never, never, *never* tell Jessica about this. Or anybody else."

"How can I get her out if I don't tell the security people in the mall?"

"Well, if you have to—tell them. But not Jessica."

Elizabeth sighed and escorted a tearful Lila Fowler through the mall, past Lisette's, and toward the door marked Mall Security.

When she walked in, she heard Jessica's heart-rending sobs and immediately felt like crying herself. For once in her life, Jessica was being tormented for something she hadn't done.

"Jessica!" Elizabeth called out.

"Liz! Liz!" Through a door and down a corridor Jessica raced, terrified, weeping, and frightened half out of her mind. She rushed into her sister's arms and hung on for dear life. "Thank God you're here!"

Right behind her came a sturdy matron and two large men, all wearing brown uniforms with gold badges and the words Mall Security stitched across their jacket pockets.

"No, you don't," the matron yelled, grabbing Jessica's wrist.

"Don't lose her," said a mall guard, moving forward aggressively.

"It's OK—I got her," said the matron. Then, staring at Elizabeth, she continued, "I think."

Stepping back for a moment, she studied Jessica from head to toe. "This is the one," said the matron. "She was wearing those Jordache jeans."

The next second, there was a bustle at the door and in walked the salesclerk from Lisette's.

"I see you picked up my little shoplifter," she said, pointing to Elizabeth.

"Not that one—this one," said the matron.

The salesclerk looked from one to the other and back again. "Lord in heaven," she gasped. "It's a regular gang!"

Jessica began crying uncontrollably again. "Liz, please tell them I'm not a shoplifter! I didn't take anything."

"Listen," said Elizabeth, "she's telling the truth."

"I saw her in the mall twice before this," the salesclerk said.

"Did you see her take anything?"

"She walked away, and the next minute I

saw a bracelet was missing. And she was here another time before that."

"That was me," said Elizabeth. "Both times."

Jessica stopped crying and looked up, stunned. "Lizzie—you?"

The matron dropped Jessica's wrist and grabbed hold of Elizabeth's.

"I told you it was this one," said the salesclerk. "It's those shifty eyes."

"Oh, stop it," said Elizabeth. "*I* didn't steal anything either."

The salesclerk's eyes narrowed as she moved closer to Elizabeth. "Oh, so I suppose nobody stole over six hundred dollars worth of imports from my shop?"

Jessica gasped. "Six hundred dollars!"

"I think I can clear this up for you," said Elizabeth. "But you've got to let my sister go. She's totally innocent—I swear."

"OK, but if she goes, you stay," said the suspicious salesclerk.

"Jess, I want you to wait in the car for me," said Elizabeth. "And keep this to yourself."

"Oh, thank you, Liz. Come on, Lila."

"Lila will stay with me," Elizabeth said.

"Oh," said Jessica. "Well—OK. Fine. I'll see you." And without even a quick look around, Jessica was gone, not in the least bit interested in anything but her own freedom.

The sturdy matron moved a chair over in front of the door, put it down, and sat, waiting. The guard moved in front of the other door and crossed his burly arms, waiting. The salesclerk from Lisette's paced the floor, watching, waiting.

"Well?" said the guard at last.

"Lila, haven't you got something to tell these people?" Elizabeth prodded.

Lila Fowler took two steps away from the wall, opened her mouth to speak, and fainted onto the floor.

Eleven

"Where am I?" asked Lila, opening her eyes and looking up at the people surrounding her.

"At the mall," Elizabeth said anxiously. "It'll be all right. Your father's on his way."

"What?" said Lila, sitting up. "Does he have to know?"

"The shop is pressing charges," said Elizabeth, and Lila fell into Elizabeth's arms, weeping.

It seemed an eternity for Elizabeth as she held the sobbing Lila Fowler under the frowning glare of the security guards. Finally, the door opened, and there was George Fowler, looking deeply concerned.

"Where's my daughter?" he said, walking in.

"Daddy!" Lila cried, rushing into his arms. She buried her face in his chest and wept, shaking with great racking sobs. "Daddy, thank God you're here!"

"Calm down, sweetheart," Mr. Fowler said, his face lined with worry. He led her to a chair beside Elizabeth where she sat down.

"Oh, Daddy . . ." Lila turned away and covered her face with her hands.

Mr. Fowler motioned to the matron, the guard, and the salesclerk, and the four of them promptly walked into a back office. Elizabeth could hear them talking in low tones as she tried unsuccessfully to soothe Lila and field her unending questions.

"What are they saying, Liz? Is everyone going to find out? What about Jess?"

"Please, Lila," Elizabeth murmured over and over. "I think things will be OK."

She strained to hear the conversation in the other room.

"Yes, yes—I'll take care of it," Elizabeth heard Mr. Fowler say. "All right. Yes, I'll make sure she's there."

They came out again, and Mr. Fowler took Lila's hand. "Come on, honey. We're going home."

Mr. Fowler turned to Elizabeth. "Well, Elizabeth, I owe you a great deal, it seems."

"Oh, no, Mr. Fowler."

"Yes, I do. And so does Lila. How can we repay you? Is there anything I can do for you?"

Elizabeth felt her face burning. Before she knew what she was saying, it was out. "Spend more time with Lila, Mr. Fowler."

"What?"

A stifled cry escaped from Lila. She turned and rushed to Elizabeth, hugged her very hard, and then hurried out of the room.

"Lila—wait," said Mr. Fowler, going after her.

Elizabeth glanced at the guard, the matron, and the salesclerk.

"May I leave?" she said hesitantly.

"Yes, and please excuse our accusations," the guard offered apologetically. "We were anxious to stop the thefts, and I'm afraid we jumped too quickly."

"That's all right," Elizabeth responded graciously, "but is Lila Fowler in a lot of trouble? She's not a bad person, you know. She's just—"

"No," the matron assured her. "This is a first offense, and Mr. Fowler seems to be a solid parent. We've agreed on the necessary steps to take, but I think you should let your friend explain them."

Elizabeth nodded, somewhat relieved, and walked out into the bustling mall.

One problem remained—her promise to Lila never to tell anybody what had happened at the mall. How could she keep a secret like that from her twin?

Jessica was waiting in the car when Elizabeth got there, and she was burning with curiosity. She had seen Mr. Fowler arrive and had seen him and Lila leave. When Elizabeth opened the car door, Jessica wasted no time. She pounced like a ravenous lion.

"Elizabeth, I've been going totally crazy waiting! What happened?"

"Nothing. It's straightened out."

Jessica's face first registered shock, then disbelief, then frustrated fury at such an idiotically impossible answer.

"I get accused of being a thief, and you tell me *nothing*?" she raged.

"It's all cleared up, and Lila went home with her father, that's all."

"Ahhhhooooooooouuuuuuuu!" Jessica wailed in indignation, stomping her feet furiously against the floorboards of the car. "Elizabeth Wakefield, you've got to tell me everything! I'm your sister! Your identical twin! I'm practically a part of you!"

"Let's go home, Jessie. If you want to know any more, ask Lila."

"Lila is my friend! How dare you keep secrets from me about her? You tell me! Was *she* the shoplifter? I can't believe that! She's rich enough to buy the whole mall!"

The drive home in the tiny little car was a nightmare, as somehow Elizabeth held off Jessica's unending barrage of questions.

"I'll find out from Lila!" Jessica finally shrieked.

"That's the idea," Elizabeth said with what Jessica considered maddening calm. Jessica leaped from the car, slammed the door, and stalked into the house.

"What a day!" Elizabeth said, then sighed as she followed her twin into the house.

The next morning Jessica would not talk to her, but Elizabeth wasn't too heartbroken. She didn't expect it to last. If there was one thing she could be sure of, it was that Jessica would not stay quiet for long. She wondered what it was going to take to break the silence.

The next day Elizabeth drove to the jeweler's shop, where she finally bought Todd's watchband. Feeling a little funny, she stopped by the window of Lisette's. The saleslady spotted her and waved an unenthusiastic hello. *I guess she's still not sure of me*, Elizabeth mused sadly.

When she reached home, the phone was ringing, and she raced to answer it. It was Lila. Apologetic and with a note of fear in her voice, Lila explained that she would need Elizabeth to go to juvenile hall with her and her father late the following afternoon.

Parking behind the white, Spanish-style mansion, Elizabeth marveled at Fowler Crest, the sprawling Fowler estate. Its sculptured, landscaped grounds, blood-red brick-tiled courtyard, and the fountain containing rare tropical fish were truly magnificent. How odd that Lila wasn't happy in such luxurious surroundings.

On the drive to juvenile hall, Elizabeth sat in the backseat with Lila. Lila was pale, yet she seemed curiously calm and serene. Her dangerous gamble had finally made her father notice her, Elizabeth observed.

Mr. Fowler sat in front, next to the chauffeur, but he continually looked around to smile reassuringly at Lila. He reached back once to pat her hand.

"It's going to be all right, sweetheart," he said softly. "We're going to make everything right."

At juvenile hall in downtown Sweet Valley, they met Mr. Fowler's lawyer, a slim, gray-suited man with a mustache. The four of them walked in through a side door and down a corridor to the chambers of Juvenile Judge Herbert Mancuso. They sat in deep, rich leather chairs as the judge looked over a sheaf of legal papers, mumbling and nodding. Finally he looked up, an understanding smile on his face.

The lawyer introduced Mr. Fowler, Lila, and Elizabeth to the judge, explaining that Elizabeth was a schoolmate of Lila's and was there as a character witness.

Elizabeth kept her statement brief. She told the judge in all honesty that Lila was not a troublemaker and she had never known her to do anything dishonest before this.

"Well," he said. "Do I understand the defendant in this matter has made a complete statement and that restitution has been made?"

"Yes, Your Honor," responded the lawyer.

"Would you like to say anything, young lady?" Judge Mancuso went on.

"No, sir," Lila said in a tiny, faraway voice.

"I'm sure you've learned your lesson, Miss Fowler. Mr. Fowler, I'm going to release your daughter into your custody. It would serve no useful purpose to take any other action. If your daughter remains out of trouble for six months, the matter will be dismissed. Six months probation."

And that was that. They filed back out through the side door, got into Mr. Fowler's silver Mercedes, and the chauffeur drove them away.

"Well, that wasn't so bad, was it?" said Mr. Fowler.

Silence from Lila.

"Listen, what do you say we all have an early dinner at the Palomar House?" he said brightly.

The Palomar House! Elizabeth thrilled at the thought of going to the poshest restaurant in Sweet Valley. After the chauffeur dropped them off, the maître d' greeted Mr. Fowler by name and showed Elizabeth, Lila, and her father to a plush banquette in the main room under an immense chandelier. Exquisitely designed silverware was arranged beside each gold-rimmed plate.

They ordered shrimp scampi, baby lamb chops, asparagus tips, and chocolate souffle, then topped off the dinner with a perfectly heavenly cappuccino. Elizabeth rode back home stuffed and happy, promising again on the way to a nervous Lila that she would never reveal what had happened.

As the Fowler car pulled away from Elizabeth's house after dropping her off, she saw with a rush of anxiety that Jessica was looking out the window. The moment Elizabeth opened the door, Jessica was on her.

"Where were you with Lila Fowler?"

"She just gave me a ride home, Jess."

"You are the most disgusting liar since Pinocchio! Your nose is going to grow leaves! Where were you?"

"I told you."

Jessica was shaking with frustration. "I can't stand it! You and Lila are up to something, and you won't tell me! I can't stand other people having secrets!"

Jessica was still howling when Elizabeth disappeared up the stairs. It was the end of the shoplifting episode, Elizabeth fervently hoped. It was time to get on with her own life, which had recently been slipping away from her.

That night she went out on a date with Todd and gave him his watchband.

"Welcome back," he said when he kissed her. "I've missed you."

"Oh, me, too, Todd." Elizabeth sighed. She put her hand on his cheek. "I love to be with you like this."

Todd tightened his hold on her, feeling the warmth of her body. "How about like this?" he asked huskily as he ran his hand over her back, sending chills all the way through her.

"Even better," she replied, then kissed him deeply.

*   *   *

The next day Elizabeth plunged into the stack of work that had been piling up on her desk in the *Oracle* office. A story about mid-term cheerleader tryouts had to be written at top speed. Typing the names of the girls who were trying out, Elizabeth almost flipped when she saw it.

Robin Wilson's name was on the list.

Twelve

If there was one thing Jessica Wakefield found totally unbearable, it was her twin sister's Cheshire-cat grin. It meant that Elizabeth knew something Jessica didn't know, and that was enough to drive Jessica into a screaming, clawing tantrum.

The day started with Elizabeth wearing that absolutely exasperating Cheshire-cat face.

"Elizabeth Wakefield, you stop that."

"Stop what?"

"Stop looking like that. What do you know that I don't know? Don't deny it, you creep! What is it?"

Elizabeth drank her orange juice, munched on her toast, and smiled. "You'd know something, too, if you read the paper once in a while."

Jessica snatched up *The Sweet Valley News* and searched through it frantically. *Nothing but the usual hundred and thirty-seven disasters and boring business and politics*, she said to herself.

Elizabeth was finishing up her toast when she finally offered, "I mean our newspaper—*The Oracle*."

"*The Oracle*?" Jessica pounced on it, devouring the six pages in record time. When she saw *it*, she practically fell off her chair.

"Oh, no!"

"Yes, Jessie, it looks like you've got competition on the cheerleading squad. Robin Wilson."

Jessica threw the paper under the table with a flourish and crossed her arms. "Who said she could try out?"

"Anybody can try out, Jessie. The Pi Betas don't control that."

"But she's a—space cadet, Liz! Have you seen her walking around like something out of a horror movie?"

"I've seen her, Jess. And a lot of other people are seeing her these days, too."

"What do you mean?"

"I mean she's getting popular in a big way

123

since she lost all that weight and did herself over. And she doesn't act like a space cadet, either!"

"I don't think it's a bit fair," Jessica pouted, reluctantly admitting Elizabeth was right. "I mean, a few weeks ago I could see she was a little less of a slob, but how could she possibly get so good-looking so fast? I mean we're talking about Tubby here."

"Well, she's been working hard at it," Elizabeth pointed out. "Haven't you noticed that? She deserves to look gorgeous."

"Oh, keep quiet for once!"

"I saw Bruce Patman drooling over her the other day after school."

"Bruce Patman is the jerkiest person in thirty-seven states *and* Mexico," Jessica fumed. "And anyway, what does he know? Beauty is only skin deep, Liz. Just remember that. It's what's underneath that really counts. And underneath, Robin Wilson is a deranged freak! Why she doesn't like any of us after all we did for her, I'll never know. But it's the mark of a sick person."

What the Pi Betas had unintentionally done for Robin certainly was remarkable, Elizabeth had to admit. She had not simply avenged herself by losing weight. Robin had gone through a complete transformation. The old tent dresses had slowly disappeared, replaced with flattering and stylish outfits. The pale face had taken on a healthy glow, and all in all a totally new Robin Wilson was dazzling Sweet Valley High. There were many kids, in fact, who swore she'd just moved to town. They'd never even noticed her before.

And it all started to come together the week of cheerleader tryouts.

On Monday Robin showed up in designer jeans, a rainbow top, and a new hairstyle. Lip gloss and perfect eye makeup created an effect that almost caused Bruce Patman to walk into the gym door.

"Who was that?" he gasped.

"She just moved here from Mars," said Elizabeth, who'd witnessed his near accident. "We call her Wrecker Wilson."

"Boy, she can wreck me anytime," Bruce said. "Wow, what a beauty—awesome!"

Most of the school jocks turned out for cheerleader tryouts, including Bruce, and Robin went through the routine as if she'd done it a thousand times before. Not only was she picked at once, but she was made co-captain with a completely astounded Jessica Wakefield.

But Jessica wasn't the only one who was shocked.

"I can't deal with this," muttered Bruce Patman

to anyone who would listen. "That gorgeous girl is Robin Wilson!"

Elizabeth decided to interview Robin for *The Oracle*, as her new status as co-captain of the cheerleading squad had to be one of the school's hottest items in the past few weeks.

She asked her a number of questions, which Robin answered enthusiastically, with occasional bursts of cheerful laughter. It was the first time Elizabeth had heard her laugh in months.

Finally Elizabeth asked a question that was, as she told Robin, "off the record." "Well, how does it feel to shove it all down their throats?"

"Heavenly." Robin giggled, then she regained her composure. "Well—I don't care about them. Although, let me tell you, Liz, you haven't seen anything yet."

"You've got other surprises for us?"

Robin smiled. "I've got the biggest surprise of all. Just wait."

"I hope you're not going overboard, Robin."

"Don't worry, Liz. I've learned how to swim with sharks."

After that victorious afternoon, it seemed Robin regained some of her old friendliness, and Elizabeth was happy to find herself sitting together with Robin and Enid outside under a tree one beautiful day, having lunch.

"At first I thought you really had set me up," Robin told Elizabeth. "I thought you must have known somebody was going to blackball me. I thought you just might be as rotten as your sister."

"Come on, Robin. Jessica isn't rotten."

Robin looked at her. "You're too much, Liz. You know that? You can't see rottenness in anybody! She's the one who blackballed me."

"Jessica? No!" Elizabeth couldn't bear for Robin to be so hurt, so disillusioned. "She was your friend!"

Robin laughed and shook her head. "Liz, don't try to protect her. I know it was Jessica. I decided after a lot of thinking that you couldn't have been in on it. I'm even starting to believe you don't understand that scheming sister of yours."

"Oh, but, Robin—"

"You just don't want to face up to what kind of person Jessica is. She and I were never really friends. I used to pretend to myself that we were because I wanted to believe it was really true. It must have given Jessica a few good laughs."

*   *   *

Little by little Elizabeth began to feel that she and Robin were becoming close friends. Somehow, through adversity, a strong bond of friendship had sprung up, grown, and deepened.

"I was so afraid," Robin confessed one day. "I needed to be accepted so much that I threw away my pride and self-respect. Believe me, it's never worth it."

"I tried to tell you that silly sorority wasn't worth it," said Elizabeth.

"I know you did. And you were right. But *you* were already in, Liz. Everything comes easy for you. You're bright, pretty, everyone likes you. You don't know what it's like to have troubles."

Remembering the recent past, Elizabeth had a difficult time keeping her mouth shut at that last remark.

Being Robin's new friend proved to be quite entertaining. Everywhere they went, Bruce Patman followed. Todd wasn't pleased to find him hanging around Elizabeth, but he could see it wasn't his girlfriend Bruce was interested in. Bruce simply couldn't keep away from the new cheerleader. He seemed to have completely forgotten that he once called her the

Queen Mary. Everybody at Sweet Valley High, even Elizabeth, gradually forgot there had ever been a fat and ugly Robin. But Robin would always remember.

Thirteen

Elizabeth sat in the *Oracle* office trying to figure out what snappy news items she could include in her column. About the only important thing going on at Sweet Valley High was the approaching football grudge game against Palisades High. But that was news that the sports editor, John Pfeifer, handled. *This is impossible*, Elizabeth thought disgustedly. *Maybe I should give up journalism altogether and become a novelist instead.* She grimaced, remembering what had happened the day before.

She had been working at her desk in the *Oracle* office when Mr. Collins strolled over and handed her a letter. Her eyes widened when she saw the return address: *The Sweet Valley News*. In the corner was typed the name of the editor, Louis Westman. Elizabeth tore open the letter, her heart pounding. Finally, she prayed, acceptance of one of the articles she had mailed to the newspaper on a regular basis for months. As she scanned the words, her elation slowly deserted her.

Dear Miss Wakefield:

Just a note to let you know I have received your stories. You show a lot of promise. I haven't been able to use any of them yet, but I hope you'll keep trying.

Sincerely,
Louis Westman

Elizabeth slumped back in her chair and felt her eyes getting red. She had tried so hard, she thought. And now this—this stupid letter! Mr. Collins was quietly standing beside her.

"That's pretty good, Wakefield," he said cheerfully. "Getting a letter from the editor."

"But, Mr. Collins, he hasn't taken any of my articles!"

"Rome wasn't built in a day," Mr. Collins

said. "Keep trying. He thinks you'll make it. So do I."

Well, the future would have to take care of itself. Right now, she wasn't getting any story ideas. Deciding she might be able to work better at home, Elizabeth left the *Oracle* office.

"What do you think it takes to be a novelist?" she asked Jessica when her sister later came into her room carrying an armload of clothes.

"Elizabeth, please stop talking nonsense and help me. This is the most important event of my life."

"What is?"

"What is?" Jessica shrieked. "Elizabeth, you act like Rip van Winkle! Have you been asleep for twenty years? I've been telling you about this all week."

Not having the slightest idea of what Jessica was fuming about, Elizabeth sat down and calmly said, "Jess, why don't you run it by me one more time?"

Jessica refused to tell her. Instead, she went into an utter tirade. "How can I have a sister who always talks about crazy, impossible things like becoming a novelist? It's more than I can stand! Where are your priorities? How can a sister of mine—my twin yet—walk around in the middle of the most exciting time of my life and be so oblivious to the life-or-death battle I'm waging here? It's unfair! It's sick! If I didn't know better, I'd swear they switched babies in the hospital by mistake!"

"I'm sorry, Jess. What battle?"

Jessica suddenly switched to a patronizing stance. "Liz, you poor, innocent, ignorant ninny—the football queen!"

"Oh, that."

"Oh, that? Elizabeth, I am determined to be Miss Sweet Valley High, and you've got to help me! I think I'm the logical choice, actually, since I was voted queen of the fall dance. So does everybody else."

"What 'everybody else' do you mean?"

"Why, everybody! Lila and Cara and all the Pi Betas. And most of the football team. If you want to know, I think every guy on the offensive line is in love with me!" Jessica giggled.

"Is it possible you've encouraged them, Jessie?"

"What? No! Well, I'm not unfriendly, Liz. There's no sense in that. I think a girl can be friendly and nice to several boys."

"The whole football team?"

"Not the *whole* team. I haven't dated a single boy who isn't on the first string."

Elizabeth smiled. "Oh, well, as long as you're selective."

"Well, I do it for team spirit," said Jessica. "Every one of them appreciates it, too!"

"I'm sure. So how can I help you?"

"Well . . ." Jessica grew totally serious. "First, there's the vital choice of what I should wear each day leading up to the day of the vote. The whole student body votes on this, you know. Anyway, what do you think of my new Jordache jeans for Monday?"

"You look terrific in them."

"And my cheerleading outfit on Tuesday."

"You mean wear it to class? Won't that attract a lot of attention?"

"What in the world is wrong with you, Liz? That's the entire idea."

The wardrobe decisions took two hours, and after endless switches and changes, Jessica finally was satisfied.

"Now—about my publicity campaign," she said.

"Your what?"

"When you write up all the contestants, I want you to lose their photographs, see? Give them to me, and I'll burn them."

"Jessica!"

"What?"

"What about Lila Fowler? Isn't she running, too?"

134

"Lila doesn't have a sister who's practically the editor of *The Oracle*. She'll understand."

Jessica smiled expectantly at Elizabeth.

"Jessica—no! I'll treat all contestants exactly the same."

"That's the unfairest thing I've ever heard in my life," Jessica shouted, running out and slamming the door behind her.

Lila caught up with Elizabeth after their last classes the next day and walked her to the newspaper office. She talked shyly about how she appreciated all Elizabeth had done.

"Oh, don't be silly. I didn't do anything."

"Daddy took me to Sacramento in the company Learjet," said Lila. "It was super!" Then she sighed. "He's going to be frantically busy for the next couple of months, but maybe after that. . . ."

Elizabeth said nothing. A couple of months! She could see it starting all over. Once again poor Lila was going to be starved for her father's attention.

"I just wanted to tell you how much better I feel. And I really want to thank you for not telling a soul. Did Jessica ask you anything?"

Elizabeth shook her head in dismay. "Did Jessica ask? Lila, is the Pacific wet?" They both laughed. "Luckily she got so involved in the cheerleading business that she forgot to keep after me."

"I don't know how you can ever be a writer, Liz, when you're able to keep a story like that to yourself."

The old Lila was coming through again, and Elizabeth suddenly wondered how friendly Lila would remain with the only girl at Sweet Valley who knew her secret.

The next two weeks were a supercharged time at Sweet Valley, as every beauty who ever coveted the title of Miss Sweet Valley High went into high gear. Comfortable overalls disappeared. Sneakers went into the closet. With carefully dressed hopefuls lounging around on the school lawn, leaning against the white oak trees, Sweet Valley High looked like a spread from a fashion magazine.

Jordache jeans were challenged by Calvin Kleins. Miniskirts were seen next to tapered slacks. Makeup and new hairstyles turned the young women into *Glamour* models.

And leading all the challengers was Jessica Wakefield, whose natural beauty, sparkling blue-green eyes, sun-streaked blond hair, and terrific figure stood out no matter what look she went for. The backfield of the football team suddenly began wearing sweat shirts with Jessica's name emblazoned on them.

"Aren't they sweet, those crazy guys," Jessica said to everyone she passed.

And then, one day a typewritten sign appeared on bulletin boards all over the school:

CHALLENGE ACCEPTED

It has come to my attention that members of Pi Beta Alpha have forbidden any girl who is not a member to go out for Miss Sweet Valley High. I know all about the PBAs. They blackballed me. I accept their challenge. I ask for your vote.

Robin Wilson

The sign created a sensation. People were talking about it everywhere, up and down the stairways, all over the lunchroom, buzzing across the auditorium, and even into the football team's locker room.

"Did you hear what the Pi Betas did to Robin?"

"Those snobs!"

"But that's totally stupid," Lila said defensively. "How could we forbid anybody from running?"

It was the talk of the school for days. No matter how much the Pi Betas protested that they had not forbidden anyone anything, the accusation hung in the air.

Finally, gathered in front of the school one morning, Lila, Cara, and Jessica all demanded that Robin publicly announce who among the Pi Betas had said such a stupid thing.

"Sure," said Robin. "I'll tell you—just as soon as you tell me who blackballed me."

"But that's secret," Jessica protested. She couldn't for the life of her understand why anyone would tell the whole school that she'd been blackballed. Hadn't she *any* pride?

"Well, then, my information is secret, too."

And she walked into the school.

It was the kind of low, sneaky trick that the Pi Betas were unprepared for. They knew how to dish it out, but they had no idea how to take it. They waited desperately for the rest of the school to see the light and to reject Robin Wilson the way she deserved to be rejected. But when Bruce Patman began following Robin around, uncharacteristically falling all over her, and the boys in the Chemistry Club, led by Allen Walters, announced they were naming their latest formula the Robin Reaction, the Pi Betas realized they were losing. Then, when the defensive line of the Sweet Valley High Gladiators announced that from now on they would be known as the Blackball Brigade, the Pi Betas knew they had lost.

"This is unforgivable!" screamed Jessica to Elizabeth. "You've got to write an editorial!"

"About what?"

"You're a Pi Beta, too!"

"In this contest, Jessica, I'm a newspaper-woman. I'm neutral."

"Neutral? Neutral! How can you be neutral when your exact likeness is being stabbed, mutilated, and betrayed?"

Friday—voting day for Miss Sweet Valley High—finally arrived, and the ballot boxes on every floor of the school were clogged with ballots. It was the biggest turn-out anyone could remember.

Right up until the ballot boxes were closed at the end of school on Friday, kids chanted and rallied for their favorites. The Gladiators' offensive line and backfield paraded through the lunchroom carrying a big banner: Jessica is Just Right!

Then the defensive line came through the auditorium with a huge placard: Robin Has Us Throbbin'.

Saturday's homecoming game between Sweet

Valley High and the Palisades High Pumas was billed as a grudge match because both teams were undefeated. Sportswriters and radio reporters in the Valley had hyped the game all week, so everyone was interested.

Louis Westman, school editor of *The Sweet Valley Daily News*, came out to cover the big game, and the local television station, KSVH, sent a crew. And of course, Allen Walters, the *Oracle* photographer, and John Pfeifer, the *Oracle* sports editor, were all over the place covering everything.

Hurrying into the area behind the stands, Elizabeth ran into Louis Westman.

"Never saw such a mob scene," said Westman. "I'm going to be swamped."

Elizabeth heard opportunity knocking. "Do you want some help, Mr. Westman?" she said eagerly. "I'm covering the Miss Sweet Valley High contest for *The Oracle*. Would you like me to do a story for you, too?"

"Miss Wakefield, you're a lifesaver," he said. "See me after the game."

"You bet I will," Elizabeth blurted out, her spirits soaring.

No one ever knew who Miss Sweet Valley High was before the game, because the counting of ballots traditionally started with the kickoff of the homecoming game. And the winner was always announced at half-time.

Jessica sat behind the team bench with the other contestants, waiting. Her mind was racing as she watched the Gladiators pull ahead 7–0 on a long run by Ken Matthews, the team captain.

I want to thank all my friends. . . .

Then the Pumas recovered a fumble deep in Gladiator territory and tied the game 7–7.

I hope I can be a credit to the school as this year's Miss Sweet Valley High. Jessica's acceptance speech trilled in her ears.

Bang! The gun went off, ending the first half.

And then out onto the field ran Enid Rollins and class clown Winston Egbert with the vote totals. Enid, holding a microphone in her hand, waved for quiet.

"Attention, everybody," her voice boomed dramatically. "Attention—we've got a Miss Sweet Valley High!"

A roar of excitement drowned out her voice for a moment. Winston held his hand for silence and finished the announcement.

"This was one of the closest contests ever held at Sweet Valley, and all the girls are to be congratulated for doing a great job!"

And then Mr. Cooper, the principal, walked

out and took the microphone. He held a slip of paper in his other hand. Looking at it, he read off the message.

"The winner and this year's Miss Sweet Valley High is . . . Robin Wilson!"

Fourteen

Robin virtually had to fight her way through the crowd and out onto the football field. Clearing the way for her was an excited Bruce Patman, who gave every indication that he was the date of the new Miss Sweet Valley High.

"Out of the way," Bruce commanded, shoving people aside. "Robin's coming through. Come on, Robin!"

As soon as she reached the field, a camera crew from KSVH trained its floodlights on her. Elizabeth, covering the event for both *The Oracle*, and *The Sweet Valley News* was there, too, asking questions of a glowing Robin.

"Did you expect to win?" she asked.

"No, not really. If you never expect too much, you'll never be disappointed."

"Do you have anything to tell the student body?"

Robin searched the sky for a moment. "Only something we all know but don't always remember—'Know yourself.' And don't try to be anyone else."

"OK!" Elizabeth yelled. She noticed Allen Walters trying to get through the crowd. "Make way for the man with the camera. *The Oracle* needs pictures of the new Miss Sweet Valley High!"

The crowd gave way. Robin stood alone at the edge of the field.

Mr. Cooper stepped up and handed her an armful of American Beauty roses, and Allen Walters recorded the moment for *The Oracle*.

"Procession," the students began yelling. "Procession!"

It was a tradition for Miss Sweet Valley High to ride around the football stadium in the backseat of a limousine to celebrate her triumph. The limo was out on the track, but Robin hesitated.

"Bruce," said Robin, waving him over. "Do you suppose I could ride in your Porsche instead of the limo?"

"Sure!" Bruce beamed. "Shall I get it?"

"That would be terribly nice of you," she said, giving him a dazzling smile.

Bruce raced down the field to the exit, leaped into his sleek black car, and vroomed back up the track to the field. It seemed to everyone that Robin had achieved absolute top status at Sweet Valley. She was the football queen, and now she would take her triumphal tour in Bruce Patman's black Porsche.

The car glided to a halt in front of the limousine, and Bruce jumped out to open the door. Robin walked to it, turned to wave at the crowd, then motioned for quiet.

"Thanks," she said. "And now for the procession! With me will be my escort—Allen Walters."

Elizabeth walked over to where Jessica was sitting behind the team bench. "Hard to say who looks more stupefied—Allen Walters or Bruce Patman!" Elizabeth chuckled, but Jessica ignored her. She was looking in her pocket mirror, trying to figure out why she'd lost.

"Allen Walters?" Bruce muttered.

"Me?" Allen wondered aloud.

"Come on, Allen," the queen commanded, and a dumbstruck Allen walked over and handed his camera to Elizabeth.

"Uh—Liz, I guess I'm part of the story."

Blushing but eager, Allen squeezed into the

back of the black Porsche with Robin and sat there in a happy daze as they were driven victoriously around the field, with the marching band leading the way. The cheerleaders, with the exception of Jessica, piled into the limousine and then followed the Porsche on its triumphal ride. Robin smiled at Allen warmly, and he took her hand. Everyone's eyes were on the black Porsche, but theirs were on each other only.

Bruce Patman looked outraged, Jessica noticed as she put her mirror away. She was pleased that if she was to be denied her rightful title, he, also, would come away with nothing. And it only got worse when Elizabeth snapped a picture of him for *The Oracle* in his role as chauffeur.

"Get out of here." He moaned.

"You never looked better, Bruce." Elizabeth laughed.

Minutes later the second half of the game began. The Sweet Valley Gladiators rallied to run away from the Palisades High Pumas 28-7.

Elizabeth rushed back to her room after the game, typed up her story of the exciting day, and sped it over to Louis Westman's office. She'd poured everything she had into it and spent a sleepless night after the homecoming dance worried that it would join the stack of

146

rejections she'd piled up. But two days later she was thrilled to see it in the paper with her by-line.

"What do you know!" she exclaimed to her family. "Victories come in threes. We won the football game, Robin won the Miss Sweet Valley contest, and"—she waved the paper in front of them triumphantly—"Elizabeth Wakefield has her first by-line in *The Sweet Valley News!*"

A few days later, the Pi Betas, who appreciated popularity, if nothing else, invited Robin Wilson to join their sorority. They were instantly turned down, and they were stunned.

"Can you imagine that?" Jessica said to Elizabeth. "We overrule the blackball for the first time in our entire history, and she has the colossal gall to turn us down."

"Astonishing, isn't it?" Elizabeth laughed.

"She actually thanked me for blackballing her! Even though I swore I wasn't the one. She *thanked* me! Because we made her change her life."

"Well, I guess we did."

"Well, then, if *we* turned her from an ugly duckling into a swan, how does *she* have the incredible nerve to turn against us?"

Elizabeth knew there was no point in trying to explain anything so obvious to a furious Jessica.

Robin had better ways to spend her time. After the Palisades High game, she and Allen Walters became inseparable. Elizabeth even put a mention of them in her column, "Eyes and Ears." The item read: "Robin Wilson, Miss Sweet Valley High, and Allen Walters, resident genius and *Oracle* photographer, have discovered each other."

A few weeks later Elizabeth found herself worried about how the Pi Betas, and Jessica especially, were bearing up under the double blow of Robin winning Miss Sweet Valley High *and* snubbing the sorority.

Jessica had a distant look in her eyes most of the time and kept disappearing for hours on end after school and over the weekends.

Elizabeth finally confronted her sister. "I really hope you're not brooding about PBA."

"Oh, Liz, that nonsense is about seven hundred and thirty-seventh on my list of concerns," Jessica said.

Elizabeth could not believe she'd heard correctly.

"What was that, Jessica?"

"*You* probably haven't noticed it, but the Pi Betas are terribly juvenile. I'm surprised you spend so much time with them."

Elizabeth took a good look at her twin sister. It seemed Jessica had shifted gears all of a sudden. This was not unusual, but the tone of her twin's voice made Elizabeth nervous.

"What's happened, Jessica?"

"What?" Innocence flowed.

"I've noticed lately that you've been walking around looking a little out of it, but I thought it was because you were sorting out that business with Robin."

"My dear, naive Elizabeth," said Jessica. "Those are things kids worry about."

"Well, if you haven't been hiding out because you didn't want to show your face, where have you been going?"

"To the beach. Sketching. I feel art is something extremely important to me, Liz."

"Beach? Sketching?"

"The dunes around Castle Cove are magnificent natural wonders."

Elizabeth did a double take. Was she hearing correctly? Castle Cove? That's where the crowd of college kids from State hung out.

"Jessica, are you hanging out with that college crowd?"

"I find them much more the sort of people I enjoy," Jessica said earnestly. "They understand life and art."

"Uh-huh! And is one of the natural wonders

you've noticed at the cove by any chance a college man?"

"Scott Daniels!" Jessica gushed excitedly. "Oh, Liz, he's such a gorgeous hunk! And he's interested in me."

"Jessica, does he know you're only sixteen?"

"Totally irrelevant! He's interested in me for what I am."

And with that Jessica packed up her tote and headed for Castle Cove.

Elizabeth watched her go, fearful of what this new adventure might mean for her impetuous twin.

Jessica in love with an experienced college man meant storm clouds would be gathering soon. And all Elizabeth could do was hope that the inevitable winds would not shipwreck those close to her sister—including herself.

Jessica with a college guy? Elizabeth fears her twin has gotten in over her head this time. Is she right? Find out in Sweet Valley High #5, ALL NIGHT LONG.

☐	26741	**DOUBLE LOVE #1**	**$2.75**
☐	26621	**SECRETS #2**	**$2.75**
☐	26627	**PLAYING WITH FIRE #3**	**$2.75**
☐	26746	**POWER PLAY #4**	**$2.75**
☐	26742	**ALL NIGHT LONG #5**	**$2.75**
☐	25105	**DANGEROUS LOVE #6**	**$2.50**
☐	26622	**DEAR SISTER #7**	**$2.75**
☐	26744	**HEARTBREAKER #8**	**$2.75**
☐	26626	**RACING HEARTS #9**	**$2.75**
☐	26620	**WRONG KIND OF GIRL #10**	**$2.75**
☐	25046	**TOO GOOD TO BE TRUE #11**	**$2.50**
☐	26688	**WHEN LOVE DIES #12**	**$2.75**
☐	26619	**KIDNAPPED #13**	**$2.75**
☐	26764	**DECEPTIONS #14**	**$2.75**
☐	26765	**PROMISES #15**	**$2.75**
☐	26740	**RAGS TO RICHES #16**	**$2.75**
☐	24723	**LOVE LETTERS #17**	**$2.50**
☐	26687	**HEAD OVER HEELS #18**	**$2.75**
☐	24893	**SHOWDOWN #19**	**$2.50**
☐	24947	**CRASH LANDING! #20**	**$2.50**

Prices and availability subject to change without notice.

Buy them at your local bookstore or use this convenient coupon for ordering:

Bantam Books, Inc., Dept. SVH, 414 East Golf Road, Des Plaines, Ill. 60016

Please send me the books I have checked above. I am enclosing $_____
(please add $1.50 to cover postage and handling). Send check or money order
—no cash or C.O.D.'s please.

Mr/Mrs/Miss _____

Address _____

City _____ State/Zip _____

SVH—3/87

Please allow four to six weeks for delivery. This offer expires 9/87.

SWEET DREAMS are fresh, fun and exciting—alive with the flavor of the contemporary teen scene—the joy and doubt of *first love*. If you've missed any SWEET DREAMS titles, from #1 to #100, then you're missing out on *your* kind of stories, written about people like *you*!

☐	25131	**KISS & TELL #92** Janet Quin-Harkin	**$2.25**
☐	26743	**THE GREAT BOY CHASE #93** Janet Quin-Harkin	**$2.50**
☐	25132	**SECOND CHANCES #94** Nany Levinso	**$2.25**
☐	25178	**NO STRINGS ATTACHED #95** Eileen Hehl	**$2.25**
☐	25179	**FIRST, LAST, AND ALWAYS #96** Barbara Conklin	**$2.25**
☐	25244	**DANCING IN THE DARK #97** Carolyn Ross	**$2.25**
☐	25245	**LOVE IS IN THE AIR #98** Diana Gregory	**$2.25**
☐	25297	**ONE BOY TOO MANY #99** Marian Caudell	**$2.25**
☐	26747	**FOLLOW THAT BOY #100** Debra Spector	**$2.50**
☐	25366	**WRONG FOR EACH OTHER #101** Debra Spector	**$2.25**
☐	25367	**HEARTS DON'T LIE #102** Terri Fields	**$2.25**
☐	25429	**CROSS MY HEART #103** Diana Gregory	**$2.25**
☐	25428	**PLAYING FOR KEEPS #104** Janice Stevens	**$2.25**
☐	25469	**THE PERFECT BOY #105** Elizabeth Reynolds	**$2.25**
☐	25470	**MISSION: LOVE #106** Kathryn Maris	**$2.25**
☐	25535	**IF YOU LOVE ME #107** Barbara Steiner	**$2.25**
☐	25536	**ONE OF THE BOYS #108** Jill Jarnow	**$2.25**
☐	25643	**NO MORE BOYS #109** White	**$2.25**
☐	25642	**PLAYING GAMES #110** Eileen Hehl	**$2.25**
☐	25726	**STOLEN KISSES #111** Elizabeth Reynolds	**$2.50**
☐	25727	**LISTEN TO YOUR HEART #112** Marian Caudell	**$2.50**
☐	25814	**PRIVATE EYES #113** Julia Winfield	**$2.50**
☐	25815	**JUST THE WAY YOU ARE #114** Janice Boies	**$2.50**

Prices and availability subject to change without notice.

Bantam Books, Inc., Dept. SD, 414 East Golf Road, Des Plaines, Ill. 60016

Please send me the books I have checked above. I am enclosing $_____
(please add $1.50 to cover postage and handling). Send check or money order
—no cash or C.O.D.'s please.

Mr/Ms _____

Address_____

City_____State/Zip_____

SD—3/87

Please allow four to six weeks for delivery. This offer expires 9/87.

Special Offer
Buy a Bantam Book
for only 50¢.

Now you can order the exciting books you've been wanting to read straight from Bantam's latest listing of hundreds of titles. *And* this special offer gives you the opportunity to purchase a Bantam book for only 50¢. Here's how:

By ordering any five books at the regular price per order, you can also choose any other single book listed (up to $4.95 value) for only 50¢. Some restrictions do apply, so for further details send for Bantam's listing of titles today.

Just send us your name and address and we'll send you Bantam Book's SHOP AT HOME CATALOG!

BANTAM BOOKS, INC.
P.O. Box 1006, South Holland, ILL. 60473

Mr./Mrs./Miss/Ms. _____
(please print)

Address _____

City_____ State _____ Zip _____
FC(B)—11/85

Printed in the U.S.A.